His Scottish Pet:
Dom of the Ages

By
Red Phoenix

His Scottish Pet: Dom of the Ages
Copyright © 2013 by Red Phoenix
Print Edition

RedPhoenix69@live.com

Edited by RJ Locksley

Paperback cover created by CopperLynn

Phoenix symbol by Nicole Delfs

Thanks to my two beta readers:
Nickimcc and one who wishes to remain anonymous ;)

Master Leon

R yce Leon leaned over her bare shoulder and
growled lustfully, "What am I called?"
"Lord Leon."

"No."

He took her delicate wrists and bound them above her head, pulling the rope tight. He stood back and admired her naked form. Widow Kegan had luscious curves despite having borne four children. "I am *Master* to you."

"Aye," she moaned softly.

He moved in close and wrapped his arm just under her breasts. Ryce bit down on her neck before stating, "You will speak to me in proper English."

"Yes," she answered, correcting herself.

"Yes, what?"

"Yes, Master."

He cupped her breasts, appreciating their fullness before pinching her sensitive nipples. She cried out in aching pleasure. Ryce knew she preferred it rough.

"I believe I shall give you ten lashings," he murmured casually.

"Thank you… Master."

His lips traveled to the other side of her neck and he bit down hard. Ryce felt her shift as her knees gave out and her full weight hung from the rope. He waited until she recovered her position.

"Don't move," he ordered, walking away from her.

She'd waited a week for this and he wasn't inclined to hurry. He took his whip from the hook and let the thong slowly unfurl. He watched with amusement as her body tensed at the sound it made contacting the floor. He'd constructed a special area in the barn for such encounters. It allowed for the abundance of room required for the wielding of a bullwhip.

"Are you ready, Kegan? I will not be light."

"Ay—yes, Master."

He snorted. "An extra one with bite for that slip."

She shuddered. Ryce knew if he were to feel between her legs, he would find her already dripping.

He cocked the bullwhip, extending the length of it behind him. In a relaxed, fluid motion he cast it towards her. It cracked beside her ear, close enough to cause a wisp of hair to move from the air current.

She whimpered.

He moved the handle around his head gracefully, following the crack immediately with a solid stroke across her back. She cried out in pleasure as the skin reddened on contract.

He stopped and let her suffer while she waited for the next stroke. "You crave it, do you not?"

"Yes, Master. I *need* the whip."

This was their temporary escape. She from the responsibility of being the sole parent of four starving children, and he from the loneliness that resulted from the curse that plagued him.

"I know you do… and I shall provide!" He cocked the whip again and gave three lashes in quick succession. He relished her lustful cries, watching as her body quivered with desire.

"Master…"

Her need called to him, but he forced her to wait; it made for a more passionate coupling. He set his jaw as he delivered four more strokes with added sting. His expertise gave him complete control over the intensity of her experience.

She struggled against her bonds, swaying her ass seductively.

Ryce crisscrossed the next set, leaving a lovely red X.

"Thank you, Master," she moaned huskily.

"We are not finished, Kegan."

Her muscles stiffened at his words. Oh yes, she knew this one would bite. Again, he waited, allowing the seconds to tick by, satisfied in the knowledge each one was multiplied many times over in Kegan's mind.

Ryce delivered the final blow with enough power to make her scream. His cock stirred, demanding its own fulfillment. "Are you ready to please your Master?"

She twisted on the rope, gasping, "Yes…Master."

"I will be rough with you tonight."

"Please."

He cleaned and oiled his bullwhip, taking his time as she hung on the rope. He wanted her to boil at the peak of her desire before he ravished her. Once the bullwhip was returned to its proper place, he walked over to his temporary slave and began gently untying the ropes. She fell into his arms when the last was released.

Ryce picked her up and headed towards the cottage. He had chosen a small, unassuming residence this time. Although the locals suspected he was a man of some wealth, they could not be sure how much. He found it better that way. Too much wealth and you became an outcast among the commoners and a prize to be fought over by the aristocrats.

He laid his conquest on the sizable bed, caressing her pale Scottish skin. Her areolas were a soft brown and contracted alluringly into hard buds under his focused manipulation. Ryce gazed between her legs. She had an attractive patch of chestnut covering her womanly honor.

Kegan gasped when he brazenly separated her pink outer folds with his hand. He could tell by her dripping moistness that she *needed* to be consumed.

It was a rush like no other—transporting a woman to an intense level of passion she could not reach on her own. The ability to deliver both pain and pleasure in equal proportions while leaving the woman desperate and hungry for more was a gift. It was a gift that he could use solely for his pleasure; however, that was not his intent.

Ryce's greatest satisfaction came from watching his women climax just before his own release. The feeling equaled no other, bar one…

He shook his head to rid himself of the unwanted thought and flipped Kegan onto her stomach with more force than he intended. She shrieked in surprise and then panted with anticipation. Yes, this one liked it rough.

Ryce grabbed her ankles and pulled her closer. "Stay," he ordered as he ripped off his boots. He crawled on top of her, grateful for the ease of the kilt. He held down her buttocks as he plowed his throbbing staff inside her depths. His cock forced her body to stretch, it was a sensation they both enjoyed.

She screamed as he drove the full length of his rod into her. "Take it, woman."

"I want!" she begged.

He pushed down on her hips as he delivered stroke after merciless stroke. She grunted, taking his pounding with enthusiasm. His hands dug into her flesh as he plunged into her. Ryce changed angles, rolling his pelvis as he sought even deeper access.

"Too much," she whimpered under his beefy frame.

It was the game she played, asking for more by pretending she couldn't take it. He grabbed her shoulders for more leverage and delivered the fullness of him. Kegan screamed and then became silent as she lost herself in the animalistic thrusting. For a short moment in time, everything fell away for the two of them. All pain, horrors of the past, and the cherished memories that made life unbearable now.

Ryce *almost* gave into the orgasmic eruption building inside him. He became still to regain control as he waited. Kegan's body trembled wildly beneath him, her inner muscles massaging his stiff organ as she climaxed. When her caress began to subside he snarled, pulling out from her moist depths to spread his seed over her heart-shaped ass.

He collapsed beside her and whispered, "Good, Kegan."

"Thank you, Master," she said with a satisfied sigh.

Thankfully, Kegan only sought this passionate release without wanting emotional attachment. Her world revolved around her children—they were a complication he could ill afford.

But he had to admit, the constant uprooting was beginning to wear on him. He hoped to stay fifteen years this time, possibly longer. It all depended on how long it took for people to note his ageless face. Eventually, rumors would start and he'd be forced to disappear... or suffer the consequences. The burning rage that he buried in his heart reared its head for a brief moment and he growled ominously under his breath.

Kegan, who had reached out to him, suddenly froze. He could feel her terror radiating from her.

Ryce drove it back down; his consuming need for revenge had no place here. These people had done nothing wrong. If he kept a level head, he had many years to look forward to in this quiet Highlands community—ample time to taste and tease the feminine outcasts of Rannoch. To distract him from the displaced anger, he thought about Avril, the lonely peasant with a comely face despite the deep gashes across her jaw. She deserved to discover the pleasures of a man and the thrill of a good spanking. He had a mind to visit her after he returned from his visit to the Baron of Rannoch.

Ryce turned his attention back on Kegan, brushing her cheek lightly in reassurance. "I'll be gone for several days. I have business with Sir Ryan."

"No!" she pleaded, grabbing onto his arm in protest. "The Baron is thrawn. Dinnae go!"

He unclasped her hand and placed it on her stomach. "Proper English, Kegan," he reminded her coolly, before leaving the bed and walking over to his cupboard. "I *am* leaving tomorrow." He gathered most of his food in a worn bag and handed it to her nonchalantly. "Take it or it shall go to waste."

Kegan quickly grasped the sack to her chest. "I will make sure it does not, Master."

"Fine. Dress and leave. I have a long journey ahead." He turned to spare her from thanking him. Ryce had to carefully orchestrate his contributions to her large brood. He could let her children starve; however, he could not come across as overly generous either. Charity was not appreciated; he'd learned that lesson long ago.

Ryce listened with amusement as Kegan walked to the door, noticing the extra lightness in her step. She shut the door quietly before scampering to the barn to retrieve her clothes.

It pleased him to provide for her and her bairns. He chuckled to himself. Now *he* was thinking in the native dialect.

He packed up the rest of the food, leaving only a few pieces of dried meat for supper when he returned. The trip ahead would be arduous, but was required. Ryce must pay homage to the powers that be if he wanted to remain undisturbed. Considered a Saxon by the locals, he was in danger of being ostracized or banished and required the protection of the Baron. It was an unwelcome, but necessary complication when living abroad. He had grown tired of England and needed this chance to spread his wings again.

Scottish Waif

The obligatory visit proved more taxing than he presumed. The rain started before he headed out and remained steady, making the travel intolerable. Once there, he found that the Baron of Rannoch, known as a Saxon sympathizer, was a conniving little man who craved only two things: conquering virgins and padding his pitiful frame with jewelry. Ryce was able to provide several unique trinkets to add to the Baron's collection, but was advised to procure more.

Ryce was grateful that the Baron was an easy man to manipulate, but he left the manor with a sense of unease. How many others might be pulling on the blaggard's puppet strings or, worse, biding their time to overthrow the wretch?

He hefted his saturated cloak back onto his shoulders as he left the expansive manor grounds, letting out a frustrated grunt. He still faced a two-day journey ahead in the rain. The gray haze cast a dreariness over the landscape that seeped into his soul as he listened to the continuous plodding of his horse in the thick Scottish mud. The constant downpour left everything cold, dirty—dank.

He was extremely disappointed hours later not to see any signs of life in the tiny village he passed through. He'd hoped for a warm draught or at the very least some respite from the relentless torrent. The reason for the village's desertion became obvious when he headed up the hill on the other side.

A small band of mourners were gathered at the graveyard. It was not an uncommon sight due to the recent famine, and Ryce was tempted to pass by, but he turned his horse towards the meager assembly to pay his respects to the suffering.

His boots slapped the mud with an oozing thud as he dismounted. He tied the reins to a small bush and joined the dismal group. There were almost thirty gathered, all in tattered rags. A few old men, several women and an abundance of scrawny children.

Silence greeted his intrusion. After several strained moments, he snorted authoritatively, "Continue."

A few words were said for the woman who had passed and then the mud was thrown upon her emaciated remains. All of them were likely to die the same way. Freezing rain, combined with the famine, posed certain death to the weak and aged.

A withered hand grasped the sleeve of his drenched cloak. "Take 'er. Ye must take 'er."

Ryce patted the old woman's hand. "There, there. You're in shock."

The old woman tugged on his arm more fiercely. "Ye have to take Chrisselle!"

The group voiced their agreement, all but one miserable figure who stood away from the group. The girl's hair was matted and wet, her gaunt figure trembling under her threadbare dress.

"I cannot," he replied firmly.

A skeletal woman holding a tiny babe shouted, "Ye cannae leave 'er haur. My bairns ur starving. We cannae feed 'er!" She pointed to several fresh graves up the hill.

The entire group echoed a chorus of hearty, "Ayes!"

"But I am a stranger, for God's sake. The girl needs to remain with her people."

"Nae. We ur starvin'. The lass must go wi' ye."

"I have no use for her," he protested.

"She is of age," the old woman stated, grabbing the girl and thrusting her at Ryce.

He stepped back to let the girl know he was not interested in the offer being made. She could not have been a more pitiful sight. All skin and bones, the girl was sickly and unkempt.

The woman carrying the infant added, "She's a 'ard worker. Aren't ye, lass?"

The girl's hoarse voice came out in the barest of whispers. "Dinnae make me go wi' heem."

"Isnae fur ye to say," a scraggy wisp of a man snapped. "Ye mathair is deid. We dinnae want ye haur."

Ryce had heard enough. It was obvious the village could not spare the food and now that she had no family to look out for her, the girl was certain to die. "Fine. Gather her things."

The old woman shook her head slowly.

Of course, the girl was wearing all she had in the world. Ryce was furious at being put in this position and commanded gruffly to the young lass, "Get on the horse."

She did so reluctantly, but he did not miss the muffled sounds of her crying. *God's teeth, what am I getting myself into?* He hoisted himself onto his steed and wrapped his wet cloak around her, hoping the shared body heat might warm her.

Her body was like ice. *She'll probably die along the way*, he thought, as he kicked his horse and took off.

They rode without speaking. It took hours before her sobs finally quieted. Had this responsibility not been thrust upon him, he would have had sympathy for the girl. She'd just lost her mother and was alone in the world in the hands of a stranger. However, he had no interest in caring for her and no one he trusted to hand her off to. For all intents and purposes, he was stuck with the waif.

"We will stop here for the evening," he told her, pointing to the rock alcove he had spotted days earlier on his travels through the area. He slipped off the horse and tied the reins to a tree. Ryce held out his hands to catch her and was horrified to feel how light she was. He fished out his supplies from the saddle pack and guided her into the cave, hoping it would provide relief from the unrelenting rain. It was a shame Eventide would have to remain in the downpour, as he knew the horse needed a break from the constant raindrops as much as he did.

Ryce covered her in his only blanket, knowing it would not be enough to warm her. Had he been alone, he would have skipped a fire that night, but he wasn't sure she would last until morning without one. It took until dusk to gather enough wood and long into the night before he was able to build a fire from the damp sticks.

"Sit next to it," he huffed, in a foul mood after spending hours to coax the flames. He pulled out a dried piece of deer meat from his bag and handed it to her. The girl refused to take what he offered, even though he could hear her stomach growling.

"Take it," he ordered. When she failed to obey, he tore off a small piece and knelt next to her. "You can open your mouth or I can force it down your gullet. Doesn't matter to me."

The girl slowly opened her blue lips, closing her eyes as she did so. He gently placed the morsel on her tongue and watched tears run down her cheeks as she chewed. Her reaction softened his heart. "That's it, lass," he encouraged. He continued to feed her a few more pieces, but put the rest away for later, taking none for himself. "We need to get your body used to food again."

He followed the food up with sips of fresh water. He tilted her head back gently to help her drink. She had eyes the color of moss with a depth that was cavernous to his soul. He looked away and muttered, "You'll be fine."

Ryce ordered her to lie near the fire and placed the blanket over her thin frame. Despite the protection of the cave and the fire, her teeth were chattering. No wonder, there was no meat on the girl to hold in heat. Without any explanation, he gathered her into his arms and covered both of them with the blanket, tucking it securely around her.

She became stiff in his embrace, which made him chuckle. "Have no fear. I prefer women with meat on their bones."

By the time the fire died, she was asleep. He closed his eyes, but could not drift off himself. The waif was going to complicate his life in ways he could not manage.

Ryce unconsciously snarled in frustration and felt the girl stir. He remained quiet and she snuggled closer to him, falling back into a fitful slumber.

How could he keep his secret from her? There was no possible way to keep it hidden with her living in the same quarters. The only option was to get rid of her before she had a chance to discover his curse.

"You will not ruin what I have created here, little lass," he whispered softly. He listened, and noticed her breath remained steady. He had to admit, the girl had a strong will. She was tougher than he thought and might survive after all.

At the break of dawn, Ryce woke her up. Without a word, he pointed to the horse. He was determined to get her to his cottage. It meant he would have to ride Eventide hard, for it was his intention to make it before nightfall.

The girl never complained, and ate obediently whenever he took a few moments to water his steed. He explained as he hand-fed her, "Your body is desperate for meat. It is good to see you keeping it down." Naturally, he only gave her tiny rations. More than that and it would end up back in the dirt as she retched. Fortunately for her, he'd had extensive experience with starvation and personally knew how much a stomach could take before it protested violently.

As the sun began to settle down on the horizon, the girl spoke her first words to him. "It's gloaming."

"What?" he asked, still unfamiliar with some words of the Scottish dialect.

She pointed to the sinking sun. "Gloaming."

"Ah… well, yes, it is almost dusk and we still have hours to go. I am determined to get you to a warm place tonight."

She asked softly, "Whit's yer name?"

"Master Leon, lass. You shall call me by that name alone."

"Aye, Master Leon."

He smiled at the Scottish lilt she added to his name. "And your name?"

"Chrisselle Buchanan."

"A fine Scots name."

"Aye," she said forlornly, slumping against the saddle.

He'd momentarily forgotten her circumstances in an attempt to make idle conversation. Her family was dead and her people had abandoned her. He could think of nothing worse—at least not for her.

Ryce changed the subject. "We are lucky the rain finally stopped."

She said nothing, but nodded her head against his chest.

When it became too dark to see, he dismounted his horse and continued on foot leading the animal. He knew the area well enough to chance the dark passage. He and Eventide stumbled several times in the inky black. He understood he was risking harm to his stallion, but the drive to get home overrode his vigilant nature.

Ryce was relieved when he finally spotted the cottage. "A warm meal and bed is almost yours, Buchanan," he announced.

"Ma name is Chrisselle, Master Leon."

He immediately corrected her, needing to establish distance. "While you are under my roof you shall simply be known by your clan name."

She was silent. He wondered what she was thinking. Was she worried he would harm her, or was she too distraught to appreciate how vulnerable she truly was? He decided to keep her unsure of his intentions, hoping to discourage her from questioning him. It was imperative that he find a safe place for her before complications ensued.

He had her start a fire while he took care of Eventide. His horse needed extra attention after such a demanding journey. Ryce talked to the beast as he watered and combed the stallion in the stable. "You did well today. The girl needed warmth and sleep. She'll recover because of you." He curried the dark grey flank of his prized horse. "It's a fine mess, I know. Maybe I should have left her to her fate." His quick hands finished the job and he covered the steed in a blanket. "Just a little food tonight. I don't need you getting sick, too." He slapped Eventide's shoulder when the beast nickered. "Don't worry, there'll be plenty for you in the morning."

Ryce entered the small stone dwelling, glad to see she was standing next to a healthy fire. He grabbed a pot and left to fill it with creek water, then returned putting it over the fire. "Tonight will be a meager meal, but that's probably all you can handle." He broke up the last remaining deer meat and added the few pieces from his cupboard, throwing it all into the pot. "A little warm soup will do you good, Buchanan."

The girl looked like she was about to fall over. He dragged a chair next to the fireplace, noticing that she stiffened when he touched her shoulder. He ordered her to sit. She sank into the chair gratefully, but he could tell she was all nerves.

Good, he thought. *I don't want her getting comfortable around me.* He looked at her matted hair and shook his head. There was no way to untangle such a mess. He pulled out his knife and approached her. The wide-eyed look she gave him was comical. "You cannot lay your head anywhere in my home until you are properly cleaned. It cannot be done with this rat's nest for hair." She did not protest when he grabbed a hank of hair and began cutting through it. Halfway through his butcher job, however, he noticed a tear running down her cheek.

"No need to cry. You will look a sight better without it."

"Nae, I wull look like a…" She barely choked out the last word. "Laddie." Then the tears started falling.

Ryce shook his head, but kept hacking away. He realized it wasn't just the hair she was mourning the loss of. "Hair grows out, until it does you can be grateful for the ease of care." She began sobbing softly. "Enough!" His tactics were heartless and that was fine with him. He could not afford to concern himself with her.

Gathering the pile of dark red tangles off the floor, he opened the door and threw them outside for the animals. At least her hair would be of some use.

Ryce turned back to her and had to stifle his laughter. She looked pathetic with her red-rimmed eyes, that gaunt little face and her short hair sticking up in ridiculous angles.

"First you eat, and then you bathe before bed." He took the hot soup off the fire and poured it into a bowl before going out and refilling the pot with creek water to boil for her bath. Even if he thoroughly cleaned her, it was pointless if she still wore the clothes. He groaned inwardly, knowing what that would mean.

Jovita…

He stormed back into the house, suddenly angry at the girl for causing him this unwelcomed pain. When he saw she hadn't eaten the soup, he barked, "Eat!" He said it with such force that she immediately grabbed the spoon on the table and began shoveling it into her mouth. "Not so fast," he growled, "you'll make yourself ill."

She obediently slowed down, averting her eyes. He ignored her and wrestled the wooden wash tub to the middle of the room. He made sure the water was warm enough before he ordered her to bathe. "Good. With hot soup inside your stomach and a warm bath, I am sure you will be able to get a good night's rest. Now strip and get into the tub."

The girl looked at him in horror as she crossed her hands over her chest. "Nae. I cannae!"

"I don't want you, fool! Do what I say."

She shook her head vigorously.

Ryce sighed in disgust, but realized she was in the right. "Fine. I will turn my head. Strip and throw your clothes in a pile over here." He pointed next to the fireplace. "You can jump in the tub." He turned his back on her and waited. It took several moments, but he finally heard her slip into the water. When he turned around, she was sitting cross-legged in the small tub, covering her breasts defiantly.

He strode over to her pile of rags and threw them into the fire.

"Whit ye doin'?" she cried, scrambling out.

"Getting rid of the filth," he answered, unintentionally staring at her naked body when he turned to address her. Her bony frame made her look like a child, not a young woman.

She scurried back into the tub, mumbling, "I hae neathin' now…"

Tears rolled down her cheeks again and he wanted none of it. "I have some clothes far more appropriate, Buchanan. Stop crying and clean up." He left for the barn to give her privacy and to retrieve the dreaded garment.

Ryce walked directly to the last horse stall, listening to Eventide nicker as he passed. He stared at the trunk hidden in the shadows of the furthest corner. He'd carried the trunk with him wherever he settled, despite the fact it only brought heartache and guilt.

He approached it, wishing he could prevent the inevitable, but he refused to hesitate as he unlocked the loathed trunk with the key attached around his neck. He slowly opened the lid, drinking in the faint smell of her. He closed his eyes and remembered.

Jovita. God, how I miss thee…

He saw her innocent smile, the joy that radiated from her brown eyes, those lips that knew him so well. A flash of blood smeared the vision and he abruptly opened his eyes.

"No."

Ryce pulled out the sky-blue dress and slammed the trunk shut, preventing further memories. He strode back to the cottage angrily. The girl's presence was causing him needless pain. She had to go, the sooner the better—whatever the cost.

"Dry off and dress, now!" he barked, throwing the dress to the floor beside her.

He turned away, not wanting to acknowledge the waif who had introduced emotional ambiguity into his life. He closed his eyes and clenched his jaw as he waited for her to comply.

Ryce was not prepared when he turned and saw her in Jovita's dress. Even though it hung on her like a sack and her hair was short like a boy's, she was beautiful.

He snarled with the taint of a hundred years of pent-up agony. "Don't ruin that dress, girl!" Ryce rushed out the door, unable to bear her presence any longer. *Must. Get. Rid.*

He hiked into the darkness, oblivious to his surroundings. Soon, however, he heard the hooves of Eventide echoing against the rocks behind him. The horse was more like a pup than equine.

"Go home," he shouted.

The hooves picked up their pace, and he soon felt a blow to his back—Eventide's greeting when he was concerned for his master.

Ryce couldn't stop from chuckling as he turned around and swatted Eventide. "You nuisance! I should trade you in for something more useful, like a donkey."

The horse punched him in the gut with his head this time.

"What? Were you afraid your master would get lost so you followed me?" Ryce changed direction and headed back to the cottage in order to end the equine assault. "We'll have to get rid of her as soon as possible. I can't stand to look at her in that dress."

The steed nickered as if he understood and gave Ryce another hit with his muzzle, knocking him off balance.

He slapped the horse. "Enough, Eventide." To himself he added, "She will *not* complicate my life."

By the time Ryce returned, he had regained his detached composure. There was no need to take it out on the girl. She had done nothing to deserve it. He opened the door to her frightened yelp.

"It is only I," he stated calmly. Looking at her pale, gaunt face he realized how drained she was. Sympathy for the young woman pricked at his heart. He pulled out an old undershirt and handed it over to her. "It's the best I can do for nightclothes. I will sleep in the barn. It is important that you remain warm and get plenty of rest."

Before she could reply, he ripped a blanket off the bed and exited the cottage. The last thing he needed was the local community finding out he was housing Buchanan. The community here would not stomach the idea of a 'Saxon' taking advantage of one of their own, even if she was an abandoned waif.

He lay down in the hay and attempted to sleep, but his stomach growled loudly and would not quiet. *Tomorrow I hunt*, he promised himself. *Then I visit Avril and find a home for the girl.* He focused on that heartening thought until his eyes became heavy.

Just one more day…

Naughty Seamstress

H e woke at the crack of dawn and headed out. In two hours he had killed four squirrels. Unlike the locals, Ryce had hundreds of years of hunting experience to draw upon. He gutted and skinned the animals and cooked one, tearing at it hungrily before heading back to the cottage. He found Buchanan dressed and waiting for him.

He avoided looking at the dress, choosing to stare directly into her eyes instead. "Did you sleep?"

"Aye, Master Leon."

"Excellent. With fresh food in that belly, you should be yourself in no time. I will be out today. Cook the meat and eat what you can. I'll see if I can't conjure up some vegetables to go with the rest." He held out the carcasses to her.

Buchanan hesitated.

"You *do* know how to cook."

She bit her lower lip and nodded.

"Fine. I won't be back until late. Sleep as much as you need, your body has a lot of recovering to do."

He founded himself glancing over her briefly, and noted how the color of the gown complemented her hair. He found it irritating and snapped, "Be careful with that dress."

Buchanan smoothed the soft material with her small hands in appreciation. "I will do my best, Master Leon."

Jovita used to do that...

Ryce quelled the memory. "When I return I expect to have found you a permanent home." He was surprised to see her eyes widen and tears started to emerge. There was going to be none of that! He grabbed his haversack of tools in a rush and left.

The sooner she is out, the better for both of us. It unsettled him that she was acting as clingy as Eventide.

He made the trek to Avril's small cottage on foot. It was not a long journey, although she was somewhat isolated from the community. From what he'd been told, she preferred it that way. Kegan had informed him that when Avril was a young girl, her family had been attacked by a band of rebels who'd left her for dead. Despite the unsightly scars on her face, she was a respected member of the community, well known for her cloth-making skills, but she remained unattached.

Ryce called out as he approached her home, not wanting to alarm her. He wasn't sure she would consent to see him and was relieved when the door opened. He saw a look of recognition before she stepped out to greet her visitor.

The woman was long and lean. The sun shining on her milky skin brought out the natural rosiness in her cheeks. Truly a fine specimen of a woman, even with the deep scars on the right side of her face.

"Whit brings ye haur?" she asked, her lips slowly curling into a smile.

She must feel the connection, he thought. This was going to be simpler than he anticipated. "I wanted to introduce myself. I'm Master Ryce Leon."

"I ken of ye," she said with a coy glance, sizing him up.

"I've been told you make exceptional cloth."

"Aye."

"Do you sew as well?"

"That I dae."

He looked deep into her sparkling green eyes and suggested toyingly, "I am in need of your services."

She pursed her lips in a seductive manner, but answered, "I cannae help ye."

Ryce cocked his head. "I'm sorry to hear that." He paused for a second before turning to leave, quite aware she was staring a hole into his back. He glanced back at her and nodded towards the barn. "I heard from Widow Kegan you have a horse that needs its hooves trimmed."

"Aye, Bonnie could use a trim."

"As pardon for disturbing you, may I offer *my* service?"

She attempted to hide her smile. "I suppose… She'll kick if yer nae gentle."

Ryce pulled out the tools from his sack and said smoothly, "No worries, lass, I know my way around a mare." He added, "You can return to your work. I'll leave when I'm finished."

She stared at him for several minutes before stepping back into her home.

Yes, this is going to be easy.

Ryce spoke soothingly to the sorrel mare as he ran his hands over her. "That's it, girl, I'm only here to help." The mare's ears twitched as she followed his voice. It wasn't long until she willingly lifted her hoof to him so he could begin his work. "The clipping is simply noise, Bonnie. No need to fear it."

By the time he'd moved to the second hoof, Avril had returned and was standing at the entrance of the barn. Ryce looked up and said in the same tone he used with the mare, "Do not take another step unless you want what I am offering."

"How do I ken whit yer offerin'?"

He gave her a smirk before returning to the horse. He heard her move towards him, the hay making a rustling sound as her skirt dragged across it. She was apprehensive, he could feel it like a cloud around her.

"Stand to my right, and don't move," he ordered calmly.

Avril giggled self-consciously, but did his bidding. Soon she began critiquing his work. "You're not doing it right. Don't you see it's uneven?"

Ryce looked up and stated simply, "Not another word, Avril. Otherwise, I will be forced to spank you." He continued on with his work, knowing full well what was going to happen next.

"Spank me? Nae! Ah'm nea a bairn!"

Ryce smoothed out the rough edges of the hoof with the file without commenting.

"Don't you see it's uneven?" Avril blurted.

Ryce didn't bother looking up, but shook his head in response.

When he finished with the last hoof, he spoke to her. "You are a naughty lass, and now your master must teach you a lesson." He cleaned off his hands in a bucket of water and sat back down on the stool, motioning to her. "Lie across my knee."

She looked at him warily, but moved towards him. "Yer nae goin' to, ar ye?"

He said nothing, waiting patiently for her to submit.

With the timidity of a child, she lay across his muscular thighs.

Her obedience caused a stirring in his loins and he growled lustfully, "That's good, Avril." Ryce slowly pulled up her skirt to expose her round little ass.

Avril gasped softly when his hand began to caress her buttocks through the thin material of her undergarment. "Your master must punish your lack of respect, don't you agree?"

"Aye," she whispered.

He rubbed his hand against her ass, warming it up for her spanking. He liked to prolong the moment before the first swat. Avril squirmed seductively, obviously enjoying the tease and anticipation.

"No crying out, Avril. You might spook Bonnie."

"Aye."

He lifted his hand and let it fall resoundingly on her right cheek. She squealed softly. "Naughty lass." He lifted his hand again and swatted the left cheek. This time she was quiet. "Much better, Avril."

As reward he began to spank her repeatedly, causing her to squirm against his hardening cock. He stopped to admire her shapely ass. Ryce commented as he caressed it tenderly, "Lovely, simply lovely."

He slipped his finger under the material and touched her moist outer lips. She froze when his fingers grazed her sensitive nodule. "Good lasses get rewarded, Avril." He rubbed against it with greater intensity until he had her moaning and writhing, then he slowly sank his middle finger into her.

A tiny squeak escaped her lips and then she became stock-still. He explored her inner walls with his finger, pressing deeper. Although she was not a virgin, he could tell she had not been fingered by a man before and the thought excited him. To be a woman's first with any activity heightened the experience.

He glided his finger over her moist walls, reaching for that swollen spot that would tease her to completion. He rolled his finger over the area and felt her muscles tighten in response. Ryce had her full attention now, so he pulled his finger out and swatted her ass again.

"Nae," she complained.

"I decide what you need, Avril." He pulled down the fabric to expose her naked bottom and then swatted the white skin resoundingly. The slapping sound, accompanied by the alluring way the flesh rolled in waves with each contact, aroused Ryce. It was a sensual contact for both the giver and the receiver when delivered correctly.

She moaned on his lap, rubbing herself purposely against his shaft. Again, he was grateful for the comfort and ease of the kilt. With the simple lift of material, he could have her. But he was not a gratuitous lover. He spanked her ass again, appreciating the deepening pink on her skin as her buttocks warmed to his touch.

Then he sought her sweetest spot with this finger. This time Avril cried out when he teased it. She was hot and swollen, ripe for climax. He began rubbing inside with the same motion as if he was taking her with his cock. Her body instantly responded by arching itself to meet him. *Such a greedy girl*, he thought, enjoying his power over her. He was almost tempted to pull his finger out to tease her further, but this being their first time he chose to be charitable. "Close your eyes and don't move," he commanded.

She instantly stopped squirming, but the moaning continued as he increased the pressure of his caress. There came that moment when her body tensed just before the release. She groaned as her inner muscles milked his hand and she covered it in her warm juices.

He pulled his finger out and then slapped her ass hard. She squealed in surprise, causing Bonnie to kick the wall of the barn.

"I told you not to spook her."

She turned her head and smiled. "Ar ye goin' to spank me?"

He gently replaced her undergarment back over her pink bottom, shaking his head with a smirk. "No, Avril. Now you must kiss my shaft."

Her eyes became wide as saucers. Apparently she hadn't experienced oral stimulation either. It was sadly amusing to think that because of misguided church mandates, the majority of couples fornicated using only one prescribed position, never knowing the limitless possibilities at their fingertips.

Well, there's a first time for everything.

"On your knees."

She slowly lifted herself off his lap. He opened his legs and she settled between his masculine thighs. "Lift the kilt," he ordered.

She cautiously lifted the heavy material, and looked up at him shyly when she saw how erect he was.

He went to caress her scarred cheek, but she turned away. "No, Avril. Do not be ashamed. I find your scars beautiful."

Avril looked up at him with doubt. She closed her eyes and allowed him to touch her face. He gently traced the scars on her right cheek and then the smooth skin on her left. "Both equally beautiful in their own way. You are a survivor. I admire that."

"Thank ye, Master."

He smiled. She'd called him Master on her own. Ryce watched as Avril leaned forward and kissed the head of his manhood with her pink lips. His cock responded by twitching.

She jumped back in surprise and then giggled.

"Kiss it again," he said huskily.

Avril took his cock in one hand and pressed her lips against it again. He felt his balls squeeze up tight, wanting to release inside her mouth.

"Lick it," he insisted.

She obediently stuck her tongue out and licked the head of his cock once.

"More, Avril."

She glanced up at him with a look of understanding and then began to lick his entire shaft, even caressing his balls with her sweet tongue. The momentum was building for an intense climax. Ryce threw back his head and groaned as his come erupted, shooting into the air in passionate triumph.

He was disappointed that Avril let go of his manhood, but he instinctively grabbed onto it to stroke himself to completion. He was remotely aware that Avril was sitting back, observing his actions. After the last spasm ended, he opened his eyes and smiled down at her, thinking, *Next time I'm instructing you on how to stroke and swallow.*

"Guid?"

He nodded. "Yes, very good." Ryce motioned to the bucket. "Fetch it."

She quickly retrieved the water and helped to clean him off. Afterwards, he lay down on the hay and asked her to join him. She snuggled up against his chest and sighed contentedly.

He played with her long auburn hair as he spoke. "I suppose a woman as comely as you must have a line of suitors."

She looked up from his chest questioningly. "Ar ye lookin' for a wifie?"

He chuckled. "No, I am not interested in marriage. I was just curious."

She frowned and laid her head back down on his chest. "There's not a dunderhead haur I fancy to marry. They ar all too old or too cross. I prefer livin' in ma own hoose."

Ryce's hopes of freeing himself of Chrisselle began to crumble. "Surely there is at least one decent man among them."

She lifted her head and shook it sadly. "Nae."

He snorted in disgust. "God's teeth!"

Avril laughed. "Whit, ye want to marry me off?"

Ryce realized his reaction seemed odd and covered himself, chuckling lightly. "No, Avril, but you deserve a good man."

"Ah dae fine on ma own."

"Yes, you do at that," he replied, kissing the top of her head before getting up. "Thank you for your gracious hospitality."

She scrambled to her feet, grinning. "Thank ye for ma spankin'."

He smiled and kissed her hand before starting down the path back to his place.

"Master Leon, were ye serious about needin' ma help?"

Ryce turned around, feeling a ray of hope. "Yes. I have a niece back in England. Would you be able to fashion her a dress? No, make it two."

Avril nodded. "How big is the lassie?"

Ryce held up his hand to indicate Buchanan's petite height and added, "She's thin like you."

"Color?"

"Anything but blue."

She laughed as she headed into her cottage. "I wull dae it fur ye."

Despite Avril's offer to help, Ryce was not happy as he made his way back home. The distraction of their time together could not make up for the fact he had to face Buchanan without a plan for her departure. It was more than he could stomach.

He took a detour to the MacPhersons', knowing he would be able to procure onions and turnips. No matter the level of famine, there were always those who ate well. It just took a man of means to part such people from their spoils.

Ryce hoisted the bag of root vegetables onto his back as he opened the door to his cottage. He fully expected to be greeted with the smell of cooking meat. Instead, the fire was dead and he found no sign of Buchanan. He called out her name several times, but got no response.

He set the bag on the table and ran outside, concern overshadowing his irritation. Had he scared her away with his callous attitude? As much as he resented the responsibility of her, he couldn't abide the thought of her wandering alone.

She's an idiot to run. God knows what might happen to her...

"Buchanan!" he yelled as he checked the barn and surrounding fields. He reasoned she couldn't have gone far, considering her health. He saddled Eventide and then went back to the house to retrieve his claymore, the unique two-handed sword he had crafted before he came to Scotland.

She was sitting at the table, preparing the vegetables as if nothing was amiss.

"Where have you been?" Ryce roared.

She smiled up at him. "A'm cookin' yer meal."

"Where were you?"

She blushed before she could recover. "Ah… slept all day, Master Leon."

"You were *not* here when I returned." He looked at the unruffled bed for added emphasis. "I do not tolerate liars, Buchanan."

She put down the knife and fidgeted uneasily. "I followed ye."

Ryce closed his eyes. Why in God's name would the girl follow him? But more importantly, how much had she seen? "Come over here," he said ominously, his anger dangerously close to the surface.

Her hands shook as she got up from the table. She walked over to him, her eyes riveted to the floor.

"Look at me."

She lifted her hollow face and met his furious gaze with courage.

"Why did you follow me?"

"Ah wus feart."

"Afraid of what?" he asked evenly, reining himself back in.

"Afraid ye were gaein' to leave me."

"And how would following help?"

Her bottom lip trembled. "I dinnae ken."

He corrected her. "Say 'I don't know'."

Buchanan said in a mere whisper, "I dinnae know…"

He held her chin so she could not look away when he asked, "How much did you see?"

Her whole body seemed to blush a dark shade of pink.

Well, that answers that question.

Ryce couldn't understand how he had failed to discern her presence. He was an experienced huntsman after all. He should have heard her following. The idea he was slipping unnerved Ryce and he took it out on the girl.

"I do not appreciate being spied on, Buchanan. In fact, it makes me very angry." She shifted in discomfort and attempted to pull away. His grip became tighter around her bony chin as he snarled, "I will not tolerate it."

"Aye," she whispered, tears rolling down her cheeks. "Ye wull get rid o' me now."

He snorted in disgust. "I would if I could. Until I find an acceptable home I'm stuck with you."

Ryce didn't miss the look of hope that sprang in her green eyes. "But I *will* find someone, Buchanan," he added cruelly, "even if it means marrying you to old MacDougall." He felt her shudder in his hand as he let go of her. Although he wouldn't marry her off to an old lecher, the girl needed to be put in her place. "I fully expected you to cook the game I caught while I was out. I instructed you to eat it and rest. You have disobeyed me twice today. To make matters worse, you sneaked off and spied on me. There is only one remedy for this."

"Ah'm sairy," she pleaded.

He pointed to the food. "Get the meal ready. I will return shortly."

"Ah'm sairy!" she called after him as he left.

He slammed the door and headed towards the barn. He knew exactly how to handle the waif.

Kegan & the Crop

The next morning he woke up relaxed for the first time in ages. He glanced over at Buchanan. She was curled up on the makeshift bed he'd made her on the floor. Buchanan looked all that much sweeter with the collar around her neck attached to the long leather leash.

She opened her green, soulful eyes and stared at him.

"Good morning, Buchanan. While I am out today, you will wipe down the place from top to bottom. I will be checking your work when I return, so be thorough or suffer the consequences."

"Ar ye gaein' to spank me?"

He shook his head to clear it. Had he heard her correctly? Buchanan's attempt at flirtation was completely wasted on him.

"*You* are not worthy," he replied simply. He got up, grabbed the leftover turnip from the night before and headed outside to get her a bucket of water. When he returned Ryce informed her, "I'll be out the entire day. I expect the place to be spotless when I get back." He added with a devilish smirk, "Oh, and there's a chamber pot in the corner for you."

He left with a deep-throated chuckle. If he applied just enough humiliation, she would run into the arms of another without looking back. It was a harsh tactic, but necessary. He needed to make her uncomfortable enough to desire escape.

Ryce spent the day hunting deer and eventually tracked down a small buck in a concealed thicket. Ending life, even that of a beast, was not a pleasant task. He watched with a sense of sorrow as the buck took its last breath. "Go in peace," he whispered, stroking its neck.

Its end was unfortunate, but the animal would fatten Buchanan up and still leave enough for Kegan's brood. He quickly gutted the beast and threw it over Eventide's flank before starting the trek back.

After washing the blood from his hands, he entered his home, curious what he would find. Ryce glanced around the room. It appeared she'd followed his instructions, but what surprised him more was the fact that Buchanan was kneeling on the ground with an expectant look on her face.

He had expected defiance, and wasn't prepared for this. He walked around the room, intending to find something to criticize her for, but she had been thorough. Ryce glanced down at Buchanan, with the skirt of blue pooled on the floor framing her small body. It was... enchanting.

He huffed angrily, "Do not think that following my orders for one day will have any sway over me."

"Ah ken."

"And I want only proper English spoken in this house. If you don't know what to say, answer with a simple 'yes', 'no', or 'I don't know'."

"Yes," she answered quietly.

"Always address me as Master Leon," he admonished.

She looked up at him and smiled hesitantly. "Yes, Master Leon."

Ryce sighed inwardly in frustration. This was not going the way he envisioned. She was hanging on to every word he said. He was about to chastise her for it when he heard a knock at the door.

With lightning speed, he untied her leash and ordered, "Get under the bed and whatever happens, *stay* there until I say otherwise."

Once she was out of sight, Ryce opened the door and hid his relief when he saw that it was only Kegan.

"Come for a visit?"

"Yes. I've brought you this, Master Leon," she said in perfect English, holding out a loaf of oat bread.

He hated that she'd sacrificed food to offer her thanks, but knew better than to decline it. "Thank you, Kegan." He took the loaf and placed it on the table without inviting her inside. "I have in mind something a little different for tonight." He walked through the threshold and shut the door behind him.

She smiled seductively. "A surprise?"

"Yes. I have had a *very* stressful trip."

She swung her hips alluringly. "I like the sound of that."

Ryce gave her a knowing glance. "I thought you might."

When they entered the barn he instructed her to undress. He lifted his saddle off the wooden stand and placed it on Eventide's stall door. The steed moved forward, obviously curious as to why his saddle was suddenly within reach. Ryce tapped his nose lightly. "No chewing on the leather, Eventide."

He covered the stand with a horse blanket and grabbed a length of rope, directing Kegan to it.

"Spread your legs and lean over it, holding onto the legs of the stand."

She purred as she bent over. "Oh, this *is* different, Lord Leon."

He picked up the crop hanging on the wall and snapped it hard against her right buttock. Kegan yelped.

"Master to you," he reminded her curtly. The woman was predictable—however, he was not. Ryce tied each ankle tightly to a separate leg of the stand and moved to the other side to secure her wrists as well. He stood back to admire his work.

Kegan's legs were spread wide for him. When she gazed up at him from her helpless position, the look of lust in her eyes was inspiring.

He began slapping the crop against her buttocks, warming them up for more lustful play. "I am in a dark mood tonight, Kegan. I think I shall test your tolerance."

"Yes, Master," she answered eagerly.

He watched her try to sway her ass for him, but she was too securely bound to move and only twitched ineffectively. *Excellent.*

Ryce did not want Buchanan to hear their tryst and gagged his defenseless captive. He knelt down beside her head and said, "I want to leave marks."

She nodded, moaning her acquiescence through the cloth.

"Fine." He stood up and spoke to her as he moved behind her. "Tonight I will take you where you have never been."

He caressed her smooth ass, noting its warmth from his previous attention. He would need to make it a little warmer before he unleashed himself on her. He tapped the crop over the surface, covering every inch. He made a second pass, hitting with more conviction. Kegan's muffled moans encouraged him to continue without a break.

He slapped her upper right cheek and then hit the exact same area again. She twitched and groaned. Now she would know a new level of pleasure as he took her right to the edge of concentrated pain. He caressed the area tenderly and then hit it two times in succession. She cried out into the cloth. He rubbed a new area in concentric circles and felt her muscles relax. Again, two hard strokes, one after the other in the same place. She screamed into the gag.

Ryce felt between her legs and found her soaked with her own juices. This was what she had longed for from the beginning, she just hadn't known it until now. But he *knew*. He could read women like horses. He could sense their unspoken needs. He knew when he was reaching a woman's breaking point, when to pull back and when to forge ahead.

It was a gift… a gift he'd honed for hundreds of years. It was his pleasure to deliver such attention to females whom society had shunned. In his estimation, every woman deserved to know the loving touch of a man and the commanding force of his masculinity. They were like flowers—unique in their beauty. Each woman with her own flavor of passion, pain tolerance, and ability to please him.

Making love to them was the only thing that kept him sane. However, he could only love them to a point. To give any more of himself only invited an eternity of pain. Ryce was unwilling, *but* Buchanan was beginning to pull on him.

He slapped the crop over Kegan's back, knowing that it would cause her considerably more discomfort. The less fleshy the area, the more intense the stimulation. She squirmed in her bonds. He moved up to her shoulders, striking her upper back. Her muscles tensed and relaxed as he played with her. But he needed more passionate amusement, so he returned to her buttocks, caressing and grabbing them possessively between thrashes.

Then he stood back and delivered his hardest hit yet. She squealed into her gag. He slapped her with the leather tongue in the exact same spot and she whimpered. Once more, slightly harder than the other two. The mark he'd left was clearly visible and exquisite.

She cried out and then began whining.

Ryce walked over and knelt by her head again. Tears ran down Kegan's face. "Are you ready to stop so soon?" he asked.

She looked up with tear-filled eyes and shook her head.

"Once I begin, I won't stop."

It wasn't true. If he saw she was in too much distress he would end the session. However, he found it thrilled women to think they were hapless victims in a particularly intense scene. He lifted her chin and brushed away a tear, gazing directly into her eyes. "More then?"

She nodded without hesitation.

"It shall be done." He stood up again and watched her tense. At that moment she was solely focused on him. Every movement, every sound… Her body was primed and ready for the passionate assault he was about to provide.

They were in sync—she acutely aware of him and he equally of her. He closed his eyes to savor the moment before he began. He could sense Kegan's nervousness of the unknown, but he was confident of the ecstasy he was about to deliver.

His body was relaxed, his movements fluid, as the crop danced loudly over her white skin, bringing with it red marks she would cherish later, their tenderness reminding her of this night and her complete surrender.

The crack of the leather tongue, the impact on her skin, the knowledge she was not only accepting the pain but falling into it made his shaft ache. This power over a woman was a heady experience Ryce had become addicted to. It had been far too long since he'd had this kind of freedom over another. He was ravenous for it.

The crop made its way over her back, making Kegan twist and writhe in her bonds to avoid the burn of it. *Pointless, my dear.* But he could tell by her slowing reaction that she was beginning to fly. Each impact now only deepened her level of ecstasy.

He caressed her ass again, gliding his finger between her moistened lips and slipping it into her. Her walls were slippery with her molten desire. He stimulated her sensitive spot and heard a long, deep-throated moan erupt from her. The convulsion of her inner muscles began, alerting him to the fact her first climax was at hand. He planned to give her several more before the night was over.

He pulled his finger from her and moved back over to her head, untying the gag. "Taste," he ordered.

It took her several moments to respond, but she opened her mouth and he ran his finger across her tongue. "That is your sweet taste, Kegan. Have you partaken of it before?"

She shook her head slowly.

He licked his finger and smiled. "A lovely tang, wouldn't you say?"

Her eyes drifted up to gaze into his, expressing her agreement.

"Are you ready to be used for my pleasure?"

Again, it took several moments but a smile eventually spread across her face.

"I shall leave the gag off. However, you are to remain silent." He returned to her lovely, reddened ass and slapped it several times.

Kegan gasped, but did not cry out.

"That's good, Kegan." He shed his clothes, wanting nothing to distract as he took her.

Grabbing both cheeks, he slammed his rod deep inside her bent frame. She moaned loudly at the suddenness of his entry. He pulled back out and reminded her, "Silence."

He waited until she nodded before slipping the length of his cock inside her. She was hot and slippery, beyond any level he'd experienced with her before. However, he was disappointed that he'd gotten her too aroused—she was loose. He felt like he was swimming inside her when what he desired was a tight caress.

Ryce pulled out and slipped two fingers back into her. With ease, he was able to bring her to climax again.

"Oh, Master…" she moaned as her sex pulsed with pleasure.

He took his dripping fingers from her and began to coat the outside of her forbidden opening. Then he pressed his slippery shaft against her tight orifice. She instantly tensed, but he encouraged her softly, "There, there… it's time to please your Master."

He felt her relax as she gave in to his new demand. *Good, Kegan.* He pressed against her again, feeling the resistance of her taut muscles eventually give way to his need. The head of his shaft slowly disappeared into her ass and he groaned in satisfaction.

The tight, warm recesses beckoned him deeper, but he was meticulously slow as he pushed his length into her. "So tight," he complimented.

She growled softly, obviously liking this new and illicit connection. He began thrusting gently at first, letting her body grow used to his shaft's penetration. Soon, however, he was stroking with more vigor.

Kegan cried out in short, muted gasps. "Oh, Master, yes!"

He closed his eyes, ready to give her the ride of her life when he heard *her*. Ryce turned his head in the direction of the sound. Even though he could not see her, he felt Buchanan. He narrowed his eyes, wanting her to know that he was aware of her intrusion.

Ryce heard her scurry off towards the cottage, but it was too late. The interruption had ruined the encounter and he felt his cock receding.

In order to save the encounter for Kegan, he reached between her legs and began flicking her erect nodule. He pushed his softening shaft deep into her ass and growled, "Come for me."

She moaned and then tensed as he rapidly increased the raging fire between her legs with his experienced fingers.

"Come for me…" he whispered again hoarsely.

She whimpered just before her body convulsed, the orgasm almost more than she could bear. Before her climax ended, he pulled out and slapped her hard on the ass. He knew she would enjoy it, but it was more out of frustration. Buchanan would pay for her disobedience.

Ryce cleaned himself off with a cold bucket of water set aside for Eventide. He then untied Kegan and tenderly wiped her down, whispering words he knew she would not remember, but that would help bring her back to reality.

"Master…" she began, but was unable to continue, so overcome by echoes of sensations still coursing through her.

"Lie here while I cut off some of the deer I just caught."

"Nae…" She quickly corrected herself. "No, I can't take it."

"I am but one man. The beast should not go unused." He left her to recover while he began the butchering. It was a timely distraction and helped Ryce discharge some of the resentment he felt towards Buchanan. She would pay, but he had to be thoughtful about it. She was still young and was struggling with the loss of her mother, two reasons to act with restraint.

By the time he walked back into the barn, Kegan appeared to have fully recovered. She stood before him with a lustful, but satisfied gleam in her eye. "I believe I enjoy it more when you are stressed, Master Leon."

He smiled as he handed her the haunch of deer, enough to feed her brood for several days if they were conservative. "Too heavy?" he asked.

"No, I am stronger than I look," she answered, hefting it over her shoulder.

"Of that, I have no doubt, Kegan."

He watched her walk away into the blanket of night. Normally, he would have been concerned about predators, but because of the famine the natural hunters of the land had left for better grounds.

He turned and stared at the cottage. How best to teach the girl a lesson she would not forget?

His New Pet

He opened the door and heard her intake of breath underneath the bed. The fear she must be feeling was both satisfying and off-putting. "Face me."

She slowly crawled out from the bed with her head bowed.

"Look at me," he ordered.

Buchanan glanced up timidly, but not with the fright he expected. She was an unusual combination of submissive and spirited soul.

"You disobeyed me again. I ordered you to stay under the bed until I commanded otherwise. You also chose to spy on me a *second* time. Both reasons I cannot have you remain in my house."

Her eyes widened. "Ah'm soiry."

He shook his head, her apology falling on deaf ears.

Buchanan started sobbing. "Please… dinnae… do not make me gae… go."

"I cannot trust you and I will *not* suffer your disobedience again."

She wiped the tears away, even as more fell. "Master Leon, I have no one. Please, do nae—not make me leave."

"You purposely disobey me and think there would be no consequence?"

"I…" She looked down to the floor. "I wanted to see whut you dae… do."

"What I do is private. *Not* meant for your eyes."

"I want…"

He waited and then snapped irritably, "Yes?"

Buchanan looked up, ready to speak words he did not want to hear. He could read it in her face.

"No, never mind. I do not care." He grabbed the leather leash, coiling it in his hand. "Come."

He walked her out to the barn and tied her up in the stall next to Eventide. "You will stay here tonight."

He left her in the dark barn, but returned later with blankets, a boiled turnip and the chamber pot. "Do not disturb my horse and do not dirty the dress." He said nothing more to her.

Ryce returned the saddle to its proper place and patted Eventide on the head. In a low voice only his horse could hear, he whispered, "Keep an eye out for her."

He left Buchanan to suffer the consequences of her actions. Hopefully, it was enough to check her rebellious spirit without killing it. She needed to remain a fighter to survive in this world.

He settled into bed and stared up at the ceiling. The girl was a mystery. Seemingly timid, but unfalteringly stubborn. Her curiosity was a liability, but he found it refreshing. If she wanted to simply experiment, he would entertain teaching her a few things. However, it was obvious she was emotionally needy, and he couldn't handle that. Tomorrow he would question her further to determine what kind of man would be best. Of course, the challenge would be to find a man to meet those needs in Rannoch.

He closed his eyes and saw her on the floor surrounded in the blue dress and then Jovita came to mind. She was laughing—that pleasant trill that made him smile, no matter his mood. How quickly that joyful memory was replaced by the scene that would forever be etched in his mind. The bright crimson covering her body. His Spanish beauty sprawled out on the ground, opened up from chest to groin, the look of agony frozen on her face for all time, and *it*...

Ryce jumped from the bed and paced. The memories were as fresh as the day it happened. He'd been a fool then. Never again.

Ryce started her day early, collecting Buchanan from the barn just as the first rays of sun were peeking out from the east. He assumed she'd had little sleep, which was fine with him. He'd gotten none.

He ordered her to make breakfast, and sat down to observe her critically. She was beginning to fill out, but it would take weeks if not months to get her to a natural weight. Buchanan had a gentle grace as she moved. Every movement seemed controlled as she flowed about the room while she worked.

It prompted his first question. "How is it that you tracked me without being detected?"

She paused and then looked him in the eye. She spoke slowly, attempting to speak his English. "My faither was an exceptional huntsman. He taught me what I... know."

"What happened to him?"

She shook her head and paused before answering. "He took sick and deid... died. Two days of a varra bad fever and he was gone." Her lips trembled and she went back to her cooking.

"How long ago?"

She whispered, "Seven winters."

"How old are you, Buchanan?"

Her shoulders slumped when she answered. "Past marrying age, way past."

"Why didn't you marry?"

"No men."

He nodded. The recent wars plaguing Scotland had decimated the male population. "I am not sure I will have any more luck, but I will try to do right by you."

She looked at him hopefully. "Ye… you're not married?"

"Nor do I want to be," he said coldly.

She nodded and went back to her work. She shocked him when she had the nerve to ask, "Master Leon, are ye… you going to marry Avril or Kegan?"

He glared at her without answering.

She finished up the meal and slid the plate over to him. He picked up his fork and ate in silence, staring at her. He was gratified to see her squirm.

"Until I secure a place for you, you will remain here. That is, you will remain here unless you disobey me again. I am done being lenient. Another act of disobedience, either failing to obey a direct command or spying on me, will result in immediate exile."

She shivered but answered, "Yes, Master Leon."

"This will be your only warning."

Buchanan sighed. "Aye. I ken… know. But Master Leon?"

"Yes, Buchanan?"

"The way you… it's different. I… would like to know what it feels like."

She had managed to shock him again. He gazed at her, carefully constructing his answer. "I reserve such play for older women. It would not be appropriate for you."

"But it was not that way with the old man."

The hairs rose on the back of his neck. Ryce said calmly, "What are you talking about, Buchanan?"

"He stabbed me with it."

"Who was this man?"

"Agnew," she answered, suddenly looking unsure about having said anything.

The name meant nothing to him, so he asked, "Was your mother aware of it?"

"Nae." She looked away and then started cleaning up with short choppy movements. It was obvious she was regretting sharing her secret, but he was grateful to know it.

He got up and walked over to her, taking hold of her wrist when she did not stop scrubbing. "Buchanan, thank you for telling me."

She looked up at him with those deep moss-colored eyes. "It wouldn't hurt with you. I watched

Avril and Kegan. It was different for them. I want to know that feeling."

He cupped her chin and rubbed his thick thumb over her hollow cheek. "It would not be wise."

"Please…"

His loins stirred at her pleading, but he knew better. It would complicate things for both of them. Ryce answered, "I will find you a suitable man." He realized he was still stroking her cheek and put his hand down, announcing, "Today we eat like kings. I will cut a large portion of meat. Use the rest of the vegetables. I will see if I cannot procure carrots. I feel like something sweet tonight."

He left her tied on her leash with instructions to cook and wash clothing for her day's assignment. He felt certain she would follow orders without the collar and leash, but he wanted her to be reminded of her past mistakes.

Ryce spent the day visiting various households, gathering information and making trades. He saw to it that the trades were slightly in favor of the other side, wanting to pass on his wealth without being obvious.

He returned home, more discouraged than before. Avril had been correct. A suitable match was not to be found in these parts. He was considering shipping her off to England, but the idea was extreme and potentially hazardous.

Ryce was surprised to see a basket sitting at his doorstep. He stooped down and picked it up before heading inside. Although the smell of roasting meat greeted his nostrils, Buchanan was nowhere to be seen. "Buchanan," he barked.

She emerged from under the bed, relief easy to read on her face.

"What happened?"

"I do not know who, Master Leon, but some woman knocked on the door and would not leave."

Ryce lifted the cover off the basket and found two neatly folded dresses. He smiled to himself. *Avril.*

"I commend you for not giving yourself away." He pulled out one of the simple gowns and held it out to her. "Turns out she was leaving something for you."

She tentatively took it and held it before her. "For me?" she questioned breathlessly.

"Yes. I want you to put it on now."

She smoothed the blue dress sadly, as if she was sorry to part with it.

Ryce turned away, grateful to have Jovita's dress returned to him. Buchanan seemed to take her time, and he was beginning to grow impatient when she finally stated, "Here."

He turned back around to see her holding the blue dress out to him. However, what he was struck by was Buchanan herself. She looked stunning. The simple tan dress was accented by the green and black tartan covering it.

Ryce took Jovita's dress from her, but his eyes did not leave Buchanan's face. "It appears to fit well."

She twisted in it, making the skirt flow back and forth. "Yes, Master Leon, it does."

"Turn," he ordered. She smiled as she pivoted around slowly.

Avril had added English touches to the dress, including a tie in the back that accentuated her waist even further. The green contrasted brilliantly with her short fiery hair. She was a vision of rare beauty.

His mouth suddenly went dry as he fought the feelings her looks invoked. "I will return this to its proper place," he announced, exiting the cottage abruptly.

As he walked to the barn, he put the blue dress to his face. It no longer smelled of Jovita, it only smelled of her. Ryce was overcome with a sense of loss, another unwelcomed good-bye. He unlocked the trunk and put the gown back inside carefully. He was about to close it when he noticed the flogger.

Ryce picked it up and looked at it thoughtfully. It would do. He placed the key in the lock and secured her memory once again. He laid his hand on the trunk and said softly, "You are my heart."

Before he left the barn, he hung the flogger next to the crop. Then he patted Eventide on the head. "Things are about to get a lot more complicated."

Ryce walked back into the cottage and stared at Buchanan. Was he really willing to do this again?

She smiled shyly, obviously pleased to have a dress of her own. It was endearing how grateful she was.

"The color suits you."

"Aye... yes, it does, Master Leon. Thank you." She ran to him and wrapped her thin arms around his waist. "Thank you greatly!"

He hesitantly put his hand on the small of her back and then pressed her against him. "You are welcome, Buchanan."

She looked up at him with tears in her eyes. "You are so kind, Master Le..."

He kissed her then. She made a soft mewing sound in surprise, but then her body melted into his as she responded to his kiss. Her lips were soft, supple. When he pulled away, she gasped for air.

For all intents and purposes, she was a virgin. He would treat her accordingly, taking it slow. Erasing her bad memories with new ones—possibly she could help him do the same.

He played with the collar around her neck. "You shall be my pet, nothing more."

She smiled enthusiastically. "Thank you, Master Leon."

"Are you sure this is acceptable to you?"

She answered by pressing her head against his chest. "Yes."

"You must obey me in all things, without question."

She dropped to the floor and bowed to him. "I will," she answered with open emotion. "I won't disappoint you again."

He realized that the night in the barn must have had a greater impact than he hoped. As long as he did not get overly attached, it would be a good pairing. He had much he could teach her, and she would provide a distraction from the loneliness that consumed him.

It was an agreeable arrangement, as long as he kept the distance between them. Hopefully, given time, he would find her a partner and being his pet, she would be obligated to leave at his command. Also, with boundaries in place, he would be better able to field her questions when she began to notice his oddities, as it was only a matter of time…

Her First Flogging

"**O**ur first session will be light."

He felt Buchanan tremble at his words.

"Are you ready to begin?"

She looked up at him, her chest rising and falling rapidly. "Yes."

Ryce led her to the barn, his senses heightened. He was intensely aware of her. This session was not about his needs. This was meant to introduce her to sensuality, to open her mind to the wonders of her female body in a safe and nurturing encounter.

He had her stop in front of his wall of 'tools' and turned her around. He lifted her chin and kissed her. Gently at first. She became frozen and unresponsive when he parted her lips with his tongue and began exploring the recesses of her mouth.

He pulled away and asked softly, "Have you never kissed?"

She shook her head and looked away.

"Would you like to try again?"

Buchanan nodded shyly.

"A kiss is an exchange, pet. I explore you as you explore me."

She turned back to him and tilted her head upwards. His mouth landed on hers again, Buchanan's lips parting willingly for him this time. His tongue grazed her teeth before he tasted more of her. He retreated and was rewarded with her tongue tentatively entering his mouth.

He let her explore him before grasping the back of her neck and darting in more assertively. She moaned, melting into his arms. He held himself back, teasing her, but not invading. That would come later.

This time when he broke away, she sighed contentedly.

He smiled and brushed back the hair from her eyes. "That was nice."

"Aye… yes," she said, blushing a lovely shade of pink.

"I want to show you something," he said smoothly, taking down the flogger from the wall and holding it out to her.

She stared at it with a mixture of anticipation and fear.

"Feel how soft the leather is," he instructed, taking her hand and placing it on the tails of the whip.

She played with a strand of leather between her two fingers and smiled up at him. "It is soft, Master Leon."

He bent down and kissed her again. "From now on, you will simply call me Master, pet."

She beamed. "Yes, Master."

He held up the flogger, letting the tails swing lazily in the air. "This can be used in several different ways. As a gentle caress, a stimulator, or as punishment."

He swung it in a flowing eight pattern, hitting a post nearby so she could see the action. "The slower I swing it, the softer the impact. If I want to provide a little more sensation I increase the speed and flick the wrist." The tails smacked against the post with a resounding thud. "I am always in control and decide the strength of the contact. It does mean you must trust me."

"I *do*, Master L… Master," she said earnestly.

"Today, this will only caress your body." He laid the flogger on her shoulder, letting her get used to the idea that it would soon be touching her bare skin. Ryce ran his hands seductively down her back and over her buttocks. She was still too thin, but she'd filled out enough for today's lesson.

"I want you to hold the flogger while I undress you," he instructed. He took the flogger from her shoulder and placed the handle in her right hand. It would help her to focus, having to hold the instrument of her imminent pleasure. He slowly undid the ties in the back and lifted the tartan over her head carefully, so she would not drop the flogger.

He lifted off the simple dress next and heard a soft intake of breath as he took in her naked chest. Her breasts were small, the areolas a rosy shade of pink and contracted into tight, hard buds, her body announcing how nervous she was.

"You're lovely," he murmured, caressing her shoulders as he kissed her neck lightly.

He moved his lips up to her mouth as his hands moved lower and brushed her taut nipples. She whimpered, so he automatically asked, "Are we fine, pet?"

"Yes, Master."

He began lightly manipulating her breasts as he continued his attention on her mouth. Ryce heard the flogger hit the wooden floor. He pulled back, hiding his amusement with a frown. "Did I not tell you to hold the flogger?"

She scrambled to pick it up and looked at him anxiously. He took it from her and brushed it off, although the floor was clean. "You must treat my tools with respect."

"I'm soiry."

"Sorry," he corrected.

"I'm sorry, Master."

"I accept your apology, because I trust it won't happen again." He handed it back to her and commanded her to turn away from him. He pulled down her last remaining piece of clothing, leaving her completely exposed. Her ass was tiny, but shapely.

He ran his hand over her buttocks in appreciation, murmuring in her ear, "You are a beauty, my pet. I shall enjoy discovering you."

Her breath was shallow and quick as his hands traveled from her back to her stomach and then lower. She stood rigid as stone as he lightly brushed her red mound. "I won't be taking you today, but I will be bringing you pleasure."

With the pressure off the table, he hoped she would be able to concentrate fully on the sensations he was about to provoke.

He was surprised when she asked meekly, "Don't you want me?"

His lips traveled to her ear and he whispered, "In the worst way."

Ryce heard her sigh of relief and he smiled to himself. Before long, he would open Buchanan's eyes to her feminine potential. The newly found confidence would add another layer of beauty to the girl.

"For now, I want you to give me your wrists."

She held them out to him and he lifted them over her head and tied them loosely. This first time, given her past experience, he wanted her comfortably bound. He trailed the tails of the flogger over her skin, tickling her with it. "This is your instrument of pleasure, pet. Close your eyes and let the sensations carry you. Experience the flogger's caress."

He stepped back and began swinging his arm to start a gentle rhythm. Because of her thin frame, he would only be concentrating on her buttocks this session. He hoped the next time, she would have fattened enough for a more complete experience.

He slapped the right cheek with the tails of the flogger with a resounding thud. She let out a soft, "Oh!" The second swing landed on her left cheek, thudding sweetly.

He backed away and asked, "How did that feel, pet?"

"Verra nice, Master."

"*Very*, pet."

"Very nice, Master."

"Excellent, I shall continue then, gradually building up. If it becomes too much, you can tell me to stop. Otherwise, I am going to have free rein with you."

"Please, Master," she purred.

Buchanan looked alluring standing before him, wrists bound, the leather collar around her neck, and that milky white ass begging for his attention. He let the flogger smack gently against her buttocks, slowly warming the skin up for more pronounced strokes.

Soon satisfying thuds filled the air as he found his rhythm and she found her contentment. She panted as he aroused her with well-executed caresses. Each hit sent shockwaves over her skin, building with intensity as he continued. But he did it imperceptibly, so that she would not be over-whelmed. He wanted her to crave it, to *desire* the harder strokes that he would deny her this first time. It was his teasing, the holding back that would mold her into a pet who longed for his unique attention.

He knew that her pussy was wet, he could smell it. With a mischievous grin he stopped. He saw her tense, but she waited patiently in silence.

"Open your legs wider."

She spread herself open and he lightly slapped her between the legs with the multiple tails.

"Ohh…" she moaned, her whole body trembling on the rope. He continued the light slapping, knowing it was sending waves of sexual energy to her groin. Many of his women came with that simple contact, but Ryce stopped.

He wanted more intimate contact with her this first time. He left her hanging there as he carefully cleaned the flogger and hung it back up. This next step would be trickier given her past.

Ryce untied Buchanan and looked at her fondly. "You survived your first flogging."

She blushed and smiled.

"Now I will introduce you to something a little more personal. You will need to keep an open mind."

"Yes, Master," she said with conviction.

He picked her up in his arms and carried his naked pet back to the cottage. Eventide nickered behind them. "He needs a mare," Ryce stated.

Buchanan giggled into his chest. He could feel her nervous tension. As much as she wanted this, she was still afraid. He wondered how she would do.

Ryce laid her down on the bed and then un-dressed in front of her. Her eyes widened as he pulled off his shirt and exposed his chest to her. He took off his boots next, leaving the kilt for last. It was humorous the way her eyes traveled down to his groin area and then immediately back up to his chest before adventuring back down.

He lay beside her and commanded her to touch him. Her small fingers lightly grazed his chest hair, and trailed down to his stomach, but there she stopped. He took her hand and guided it onto his cock. She gasped and then gently rubbed against it. He wrapped her hand around it tightly and showed her the stroking motion he preferred.

Buchanan looked into his eyes as she played with him.

"Harder, pet."

She licked her lips as she stroked him with more force. He closed his eyes and gave into the pleasure of it. She had a natural touch that was pleasing, despite her lack of experience. He groaned, knowing that it would moisten her already juicy sex.

Keeping his eyes closed, he let his hand wander between her legs to confirm his suspicion. She whimpered and stopped her hand motion when his finger made contact with her womanhood. "Keep playing with me, pet."

He opened his eyes slightly and saw her swallow hard before she started up again. His hand traveled back up to her face and he stroked her cheek with his thumb. "Open your legs to me."

She hesitated for a moment before spreading her thighs for him. Complete faith and compliance… exactly what he was looking for from her. "Trust me, pet. This will please you."

He repositioned his head between her legs. She stared at him, openmouthed, as his tongue came in contact with her sex. She tried to struggle out of his reach, but he held her firm.

"Stay," he commanded, before treating himself to her taste. He lost himself as he swirled his tongue over her swollen lips and teased her. Tasting a woman allowed him entrance to another facet of her. It was intimate on a primal and exquisite level.

Ryce looked up and asked, "Enjoyable?"

She simply bit her lip and nodded.

"Good. I'm going to touch you the same way I touched Avril," he growled as he went down on her again. He felt her tense and then relax as he explored the moistness of her inner lips with his fingers. With gentle prodding, he pushed his finger inside her as he sucked on her erect nodule. The distraction of his mouth helped her to accept his exploration without resistance. He knew exactly where he was headed.

"That's my good pet," Ryce encouraged as his finger sought deeper access into her warm, velvety depths and found the spongy protuberance he was searching for. She breathed in sharply when he touched it. "Let your Master please you."

Her muscles tensed as he began to caress the area. "Relax, pet," he said soothingly. All the sensations he was introducing were new, so he took his time. He spoke words of encouragement as he continued to tease her with his tongue and fingers.

There came a point when her whole body became stiff and he knew she was close. "Do not fight it, pet. This is my gift to you…"

Buchanan thrashed her head back and forth several times before settling down and letting the tension release. She whimpered as her hips pushed up in the rhythmic dance of the ages. He groaned in satisfaction. Afterwards she made mewing gasps as she slowly regained control over her body. When he glanced up, Ryce noticed tears in her eyes.

"Are you fine, pet?"

"I'm not sure, Master."

"Was it not pleasant?" he questioned.

Buchanan shivered. "It was so powerful." She added in a whisper, "Almost frightening…"

He chuckled as he petted her still-quivering sex. "You will come to desire that feeling above all else. You did well, but we are not finished." He ordered her to lie on her stomach.

Buchanan slowly turned over and lay down for him. "I need your legs together," he instructed. Ryce rested his shaft in the valley between her round buttocks. "Lie completely still for me. This is how a man comes without penetration," he growled into her ear.

He placed her wrists above her head and held onto them as he rubbed his shaft against her skin. "Come to know my shaft, pet, it will not hurt you."

He rolled his hips, mimicking the motions of fucking her.

"Your body pleases me," he murmured. She trembled beneath him in response to his words. "Turn your head so that I can kiss you."

She lifted her head up to him and Ryce kissed her, darting his tongue into her mouth as he spilled his seed over her lovely ass. He grunted in satisfaction, marking his pet with his essence. Ryce pulled away and lay beside her, liking the way she looked covered in his come.

"Did I please you well, Master?" Buchanan asked, staring at him with those luminous green eyes.

"Aye, pet," he answered with a satisfied snort. "Your Master is well pleased."

She grinned at him, her eyes sparkling. An innocent smile that caused his heart to skip a beat. If he wasn't careful, he could fall for this girl. He got up abruptly and cleaned her off before leaving the cottage to retrieve her clothes. Once in the barn he headed straight to Eventide. "I don't want to hear it."

Eventide shook his head from side to side, letting out a low nicker. It seemed suspiciously like laughter to Ryce.

"I had no other choice. Laughing at my expense is not allowed, you pompous ass." He smacked him on the hindquarter and Eventide tried to side-kick him, but Ryce easily avoided his hoof. "Nice try, old chap. Now you'll get no grain with your supper."

His dark stallion rolled back his ears and snorted angrily.

"There is a reason I am the Master." He threw in an ample amount of hay, before gathering Buchanan's clothes and heading back towards the cottage. He hesitated at the door. *Remember she is your pet, nothing more*, he chided himself.

To help keep that at the forefront of his mind, he entered and insisted, "Put the leash back on after you dress and wear it whenever you are in my home." He could tell she was hurt by the expression on her face, but it was absolutely necessary. They both needed that visual reminder of her place.

"I will be visiting Avril tomorrow to thank her for your clothes."

Again, that hurt expression returned on her face. Further proof he was doing the right thing. "Understand, pet, you and I have an arrangement of convenience. You are my property. It gives you no rights over me."

She bowed her head. "Yes, Master."

He asked firmly, "Do you want out of this arrangement?"

She immediately looked up in desperation and shook her head vigorously. "No, Master, no!"

"Fine, then we will continue on with your lessons tomorrow once I return."

Buchanan smiled at him through the tears forming in her eyes. Once again he was overcome with a disconcerting feeling of tenderness for the girl.

"Make supper, pet. Your Master is hungry." He took his claymore off the mantle to clean and polish it. This 'arrangement' was only going to cause him trouble.

Ryce heard Eventide neigh loudly from the barn as if in agreement. *Insufferable horse.*

His Pet's Pleasure

The day came, it was inevitable... Ryce unwittingly put himself in harm's way, exposing the nature of his curse to Buchanan.

He'd taken her on a ride with him to get her out of the cottage. He knew it was stifling her young spirit to be confined to his home for fear of being discovered living alone with him. A day out seemed a reasonable solution.

Eventide was navigating a thick section of fallen trees when an adder struck at his feet, only missing by inches. The great horse reared and both Buchanan and Ryce flew into the air before falling hard to the ground. Eventide's massive hooves landed repeatedly on the snake, quickly eliminating the venomous threat.

Ryce was racked with pain, but looked over at Buchanan to make sure she was all right. She seemed dazed, but slowly got to her feet and brushed herself off. He, however, was pinned to the ground. He looked down to see the sharp end of a tree branch protruding from his chest and a pool of blood quickly soaking his shirt.

His struggle for breath alerted him to the fact his lung had been punctured by the limb.

Buchanan screamed when she saw him. "No! No, Master Leon! You can't be hurt. Please, no!" She pulled off her tartan and pressed it against his chest, tears streaming down her face.

In gasping breaths he told her, "Go back… Get water boiling… I will… come."

She looked at him in horror, automatically switching to her Scottish dialect. "Ah'll not leave ye!" She began sobbing uncontrollably as blood continued to pour from the wound. He could read the panic on her face and knew of only one way to stop it.

"Chrisselle…"

Her tears stopped momentarily and she looked at him.

Calling her by her given name had the effect he was counting on. His gasping for air was getting worse and he knew it frightened her. "Do… as I say… I will… come… I need hot… water."

The terror painted on her face was enough to break his heart. "I don't want to leave ye here to die!"

He said again, his voice getting weaker, "Go… now…" He took another breath and added, "Run."

She pressed her mouth against his, her lips salty from her tears, and then got up and ran back to the cottage. When she was out of sight he called Eventide to him. The horse was jumpy from the stench of his blood, but Eventide was a noble steed and fought his natural instincts to run. The stallion bowed his head, allowing Ryce to grab onto the reins with both hands.

"Back!" he grunted.

The horse pulled back, but stopped when he felt resistance.

"Back… Eventide!"

The horse mustered his strength and Ryce felt the branch dislodge from his chest. The blood quickly filled the void, causing him to cough up bountiful amounts of crimson—the reason he needed Chrisselle far away.

He fell onto the mossy ground and closed his eyes. Once upon a time, he would have panicked. The pain, blood loss, and the struggling for every breath would unnerve any man. But he'd been through it too many times to react now.

Even as he lay there, his body was repairing the damage. It was his curse, a body that could not die. One that forced him to live on as those around him succumbed to nature's time-honored rule—where there was life, death was not far behind.

Eventide nudged him with his nose. Ryce's eyes flickered open. "It'll be… fine, old man. Just… give me a bit…"

The sun was ready to set before he was able to get to his feet. His steed knelt down so that he could climb onto his back. He held on tight as Eventide made his way without being directed. It was a hard and grueling journey, made more painful with each jolting step. He would have stopped to recover, but he knew that Chrisselle must be frightened. He hoped she'd stayed at the cottage like he'd ordered.

Thankfully she had. The girl cried out the instant they broke through the trees. He assumed she'd been waiting outside for hours hoping for his return. "You're alive!" she sobbed in relief.

He grunted with pain as he slid off his trusted friend and let Chrisselle help him into the cottage. She guided him to the bed and then fetched the boiled water. Her hands were shaking so badly that she almost spilled it on herself.

"There, there, pet… Master is fine. No sense in being careless."

She went to peel back his shirt, but he stopped her. "I can care for myself."

Chrisselle's reaction was unexpected. She sat on her heels and began crying hysterically. When he asked what was wrong she howled, "That is what faither said, but he deid!"

Ryce closed his eyes. The ghosts of her past were rearing their heads. He was unwilling to cause her any more pain.

"Fine. You may dress it."

She got back to her feet, brushing away the tears before she came to him. "Thank you, Master." She made a little hiccup sound as she tried to calm the sobs still remaining. She peeled back his shirt and gasped, then she smiled. "I thought it was much worse."

He chuckled softly and began coughing. "It looked worse than it was. Did I not say I would be fine?"

"Aye," she said in astonishment. Chrisselle gently cleaned the wound and bandaged it, asking him to turn over so she could attend to the entrance wound. "It's a miracle."

"Not a miracle, simple luck," he corrected. But now the doubts would begin… She'd seen the size of the branch, the large amount of blood. The wounds bore no resemblance to what should have been.

"Nae," she said, lightly brushing her hand over the bandage.

He grabbed her wrist and said more harshly than he meant, "I do not have patience for your foolery. Get me soup and feed my horse."

Her lip quivered as she went to carry out his tasks. Ryce looked up at the ceiling. *What is unnatural will eventually be perceived as evil.* It had played out time and time again.

No matter, he would keep the bandages on, redressing them himself, and act sore for a number of days. It was possible Chrisselle would buy it if his acting was convincing enough. *Chrisselle?* Why in God's name was he thinking of her as Chrisselle now? *Idiot!* He made a mental note to no longer think of her by her given name. She was simply his pet.

Fate seemed to be conspiring against him. A few days later, Widow Kegan came bursting through the door. "What's going on, Ma…" She stopped and stared at his pet. Her eyes narrowed. "And *who* is she?"

Ryce was reclining on the bed, but got up with the proper amount of discomfort to be convincing. "This is my pet. She is under my care."

"Under your care? You mean you're coupling with her!"

Ryce moved towards Kegan unhurriedly, knowing how important it was to gain control over her. "As I stated, she is a pet, Kegan. Nothing more."

"Pet? I see a collar around her neck, but what does that mean?"

"I care for her needs."

"And she cares for yours, I'll wager."

"Does it matter?" he asked coolly.

"Aye, it does!"

He stood before her, exuding shameless confidence. "It has no bearing on you."

Kegan folded her arms and stated, "I don't appreciate you coupling with others."

Such blatant disrespect could not be tolerated, but he did not want to incite her wrath and risk Kegan telling others about the girl. He remained calm as he explained, "Exclusivity has never been part of our arrangement, Kegan."

She glared at his pet. "But I don't condone a girl living here alone with you. It's not proper. Not proper, I say!"

"I'll not have you questioning me on this." He understood Kegan's need for correction, reassuring her that she was still his slave. "As your Master I cannot abide such poor behavior." Ryce slapped her cheek. She looked shocked at first, but then relaxed and became focused on him. "Do you understand, slave?"

"Yes, Master Leon." She added quietly, "So, you still wish to play together?" Kegan glanced over at his pet who continued kneeling with her head bowed, not making a peep.

"Yes. However, I've had an accident and must postpone tonight's entertainment."

Kegan frowned. "An accident?"

"Had you not noticed I was in bed when you barged in?"

She opened her mouth to make a quick retort, her jealousy easy to read. Ryce scowled at her and her mouth snapped shut.

He continued, "I fell from the horse and damaged my shoulder. In two weeks' time I should be fully functional. I'll need to be to carry out what I have in mind for you."

She smiled coyly. "You have plans for me, Master?"

"Yes, but the next time you enter my residence again without permission it shall be the last."

"Yes, Master," she replied with the proper humility.

Ryce was discouraged that he had no food to offer her children when he dismissed her. Hunting had not been an option and he was running low as it was. "Return in two weeks exactly at noon."

He noted her hesitation, her reluctance to leave him with the girl. When Kegan turned to go she had the impudence to glare at his pet.

"Slave, how you treat my pet reflects directly on me," he rebuked. "Apologize to her now for that look of disrespect." He then added for emphasis, "You may address her as Master's pet."

Ryce watched her inner struggle play out on Kegan's face, but she eventually turned to the girl and said in a forced voice, "I am sorry for my disrespect, Master's pet."

He opened the door. "You may leave now."

As she exited, Ryce wondered if Kegan would prove more trouble than she was worth. "Tell no one of the girl."

She looked at him strangely, but answered, "Yes, Master Leon."

He shook his head as he watched her leave. Ryce had assumed being older and possessing such an independent spirit, her jealousy would not control her.

He closed the door and turned towards his pet. He asked her to stand and look at him. "You did well. I am proud of the way you conducted yourself during the unexpected intrusion."

"Thank you, Master."

The rush of being discovered had Ryce aroused and Chrisselle's obedience had only served to fuel the fire. "I wish to teach you a new trick today, pet."

Her eyes sparkled luminously at the suggestion, but she bowed her head before she spoke. "I would be honored, Master." He found it curious, as he had not instructed her to bow.

"My cock has been neglected as of late, but that shall be remedied this moment. Take off your clothes and come to the bed."

He pretended stiffness as he lay down, grunting in pain for her benefit. She rewarded him with a worried glance while she slipped off her under-clothes. As she walked towards him, he was able to appreciate her blossoming body.

The girl was still lean, but her breasts and hips were beginning to fill out. She had the look of a woman now, curves hinted at and a light red mound that beckoned to him. He held out his hand and guided her onto the bed. "I will teach you a new way to please me." He ran his index finger over her pink lips. "It involves this." He inserted his thumb into her mouth and held her cheek possessively. "Your mouth is mine."

She leaned her head into his hand, obviously aroused by his dominance over her. He was tempted to slip his other hand between her legs to note her level of excitement, but refrained. It would be a gratuitous gesture as he already knew the answer. He removed his thumb and kissed her more aggressively than he had before. She did not resist, returning the exchange with ardor.

The girl was an eager and willing pupil. It amazed Ryce the level of trust she bestowed on him given her past and he wondered if she would be ready to take him sooner than he first planned. Just the thought of that increased the blood flow to his shaft and he groaned.

She mewed in response to his vocal pleasure and his heart quickened. The girl was intoxicating. Still kissing her, Ryce took her hand and guided it under his kilt. He placed his hand over hers and wrapped it around his cock with the amount of pressure he preferred. Together their hands moved up and down his shaft. He showed her the angle and speed that pleased him and then he let go.

She stopped, but he growled huskily, "Continue." She wrapped her small hand around his cock and mimicked his stroke. "Tighter," he ordered.

When she tightened her grip, he groaned in satisfaction. "Keep it up, pet. It pleases your Master well." He lay back and let the sensation carry him to a higher level of arousal. There was a certain satisfaction in getting himself to the point where his balls ached in need.

He felt her hand slow down and chuckled inside, knowing she was growing tired. "Faster," he told her. Tiredness should never affect his pet's performance. It was an important rule to establish. She returned to the vigorous pace and he lifted his hand and stroked her short hair in gratitude. She glanced up and smiled.

He almost pushed himself over the edge wanting to test her endurance, but coming too soon would not accomplish his goal. "Enough, pet. Come back up here."

She crawled over to him, her curiosity easy to read. *So much like a cat*, he mused. Ryce grabbed her hair and pressed his lips to hers, ravaging her with his tongue. Showing her exactly how he would take her if he could.

She whimpered in his mouth, a sound of complete surrender, and he almost lost control. Ryce pulled away, forcing his heart to rate slow down as he regained dominance over his body.

"Now for these lips to please me further," he said, tracing their delicate outline with his finger.

"Like Avril?" she asked.

"Yes, like Avril, although I am going to ask more of you."

She bowed her head. "Thank you, Master."

"Position yourself between my legs." He watched as she moved back down and she stared at his rigid shaft.

"Kiss and lick it, pet."

She leaned forward, giving him a view of her lovely ass. His pet kissed the head of his shaft so lightly it tickled. Then she trailed down the entire length of his shaft with those butterfly kisses. She followed it up by licking his balls far too gently.

"I will not break," he teased.

She immediately licked with more force and his shaft responded accordingly. He enjoyed the feel of a woman's tongue, but what he desired more was suction. "Wrap your lips around the top and suck it, pet."

Her lips returned to the head of his shaft and the warmth of her mouth encased him. "Ahhh…" he groaned. "More suction." He felt the increased pressure and groaned again. Ryce knew his verbal cues would add to her enjoyment of this lesson.

"Now I want you to grip the shaft and move your mouth up and down on it. Try to keep the suction steady. Please your Master with that mouth."

His pet used both hands to grip his cock and then she went down with too much enthusiasm, causing herself to gag. It was difficult not to laugh but he appreciated her determination to take all of him. He planned to teach her how to in the future, but for now he wanted to keep it simple. "Not so deep. Slow and steady."

She looked up at him from between his legs and nodded. She tried again, going shallow at first, until she became comfortable with the motion. The warmth of her mouth, the moistness, and the extent of the suction was causing a lusty ache. He groaned loudly this time and put his hand on the back of her head, helping her to get the depth and pace.

He watched with pleasure as those pink lips went down on him repeatedly. Again, he could tell when she grew tired and the suction lessened. "More, pet, your Master is enjoying your mouth."

She repositioned herself and started up again, matching her enthusiasm of earlier. There was no doubt that his pet took delight in giving him pleasure. It would make for a harmonious relationship. *She's truly a find*, he thought.

He enjoyed her for a bit longer and then he directed her to stop and gave his instructions. "I want you to savor the taste of your Master."

Her eyes were luminous and her lips red from their work, a vision of beauty.

"Do not pull away as Avril did."

"No, Master," she said with a determined smile.

He closed his eyes and let the sensations roll over him as she began sucking again. "Slower, pet," he whispered. He was close... so close...

The tension grew to an unbearable ache before he finally let go and his cock erupted with his seed. Her lips released their suction. He opened his eyes and watched her swallow his come. It was a heady sight, seeing a woman ingest his very essence.

After his last spasm receded, he pulled her up to him and cupped her face with both hands. "Well done, pet." He kissed her forehead and then cradled her to him, playing with her hair as he savored the afterglow.

"I'm so happy," she murmured on his shoulder.

He was content, for the first time in ages. Maybe this was why he'd felt the urgent need to travel abroad—it was fated.

The Taking of Her

A few days later, while watching his pet's round bottom as she scrubbed the laundry, he felt an irresistible urge to take her. It was as if he'd been struck by lightning and the impulse would not be denied. Being of a controlled nature, the feeling was foreign to him. Her first time was not going to be a quick, hard pounding, which was exactly what he was tempted to give her. So he ordered, "Pet, stop what you are doing, go to the cottage, undress and lie on the bed."

She glanced back at him with a charming little smile, before wiping her hands and heading to the cottage. He felt just like a rutting bull and wanted to charge her.

Ryce breathed a sigh of relief when she shut the door. He turned and made his way to the barn, stripped off his shirt and grabbed the flogger. With hard strokes, he repeatedly hit his back. The bite of the tails helped to clear his mind. There was no doubt he was going to take her, but he wanted their first time to be an exploration and gentle introduction, not the callous pounding the old man had forced on her.

He retrieved his shirt before heading towards the cottage. His mind was clear and his body back under control as he opened the door. She was lying on the bed with her legs spread for him, her red mound already wet and swollen in anticipation. He groaned. She wasn't making it easy.

"Close your legs, pet, and watch." He undressed in front of her, starting with his boots, then his shirt, ending with the kilt. Her eyes widened when she saw the strength of his erection. He smiled at her lustfully. "Today I will claim you as mine."

A soft gasp came from her lips as he lay down beside her. "Close your eyes and focus on my touch." His command was low and sensual. He caressed her skin, every inch of it, taking his time. She twitched when he grazed her toes, moaned as he lightly petted her mound, and cried out softly when he added his lips to the equation and suckled her breasts.

After tenderly biting her neck he lay back on the bed and told her, "Now I want you to do the same."

Her look of surprise was charming. She tentatively moved to his toes, beginning at the same area. He trusted that having her familiarize herself with his body would ease any fears she was having. It was Ryce's plan to be overly vocal to reward her as she explored him, knowing how that would gratify her submissive heart.

She kissed his toes delicately, the same way she had kissed his cock. It was unbearably ticklish and he wiggled his toes in protest. She trilled in response, a sound he hadn't heard in over a hundred years. His heart palpitated, the sound causing a mixture of pain and joy.

His pet looked up, as if sensing the change in him. Ryce smiled to hide the disconcerting emotions bombarding him. "Continue, pet. But do not tickle your Master so."

She grinned as she started up his legs next, lavishing attention on one and then the other. Licking, nipping and tasting her Master's body. When she made her way up to his shaft, she teased around it, but did not make contact. He got the impression she knew exactly what she was doing and how insane it was making him, but he said nothing. This was her chance to explore and accept the body that was going to penetrate her.

His cock, however, jumped and pulsed in protest to her teasing. It had no patience and demanded access into her moist walls. He took a sharp intake of breath when she rubbed her cheek against it, his cock immediately releasing precome.

She gave the head of his shaft a quick lick, consuming the drop before heading upward. She licked his bellybutton and then lightly nipped his chest. Then she stopped and moved up to his head, staring down at him. Her soulful green eyes held lust and a much deeper emotion. It was the reason for her trust, for her willingness to give herself away to him without fear.

Was he willing to return it or would he relegate her to a life of unrequited love?

He took a few moments to contemplate the question before he made his determination.

I will love her.

Ryce caressed her cheek. "You are beautiful. A treasure to me."

Tears filled her eyes. He lifted his head and they kissed. It was not a kiss like the others. It was tender and ripe with emotion—an exchange of souls.

He knew he was taking a risk, but at that moment he was inclined to risk everything. He had not known such contentment in eons. "Lie on me, pet."

She gracefully lay on top, his erect manhood rigid between them. He wrapped his arms around her and growled. "Your body feels good pressed against mine."

"Ay—Yes, Master. It does."

He ran his hands up and down her back lightly, causing goose bumps on her skin. He murmured, "In payment for those distracting kisses on my toes." She giggled, but did not try to resist his tickling.

He gently rolled her over so she was lying beside him, and then he put his hand between her legs. She was quite wet and her outer lips were swollen with need. "I am going to play with you first," he whispered huskily.

Ryce wanted her completely relaxed and ready for him. He slid his finger into her warm velvety walls and began caressing her from the inside. She moaned, now familiar with the sensations the intimate caress inspired. "Yes, pet. I want you to come before I take you."

Her eyelids fluttered as she tilted her head back and allowed her body to accept the escalating orgasm. A woman always had a choice. To remain tense and unyielding prevented those delicious contractions of pleasure. It took trust of the partner and a familiarity with the process for a woman to easily succumb. His pet was such a woman. Soon her walls tightened and her hips lifted up as she pushed against his hand. "Good girl," he murmured.

Her passionate cry caught in her throat as her body began contracting around his finger. He loved the feel of her orgasm as her tight pussy milked his finger. She turned her face towards him and he kissed her as she finished her climax.

She opened her eyes. The green color had taken on a darker hue. That was it, he had to have her. Ryce moved between her legs and gazed upon her. "I will not hurt you."

She nodded, her eyes luminous with longing even as her breasts rose and fell rapidly. She was nervous, but he sensed that she was not afraid. He pushed the head of his cock against her opening. It was already wet and pliant from her recent orgasm. He looked into those moss-colored eyes as he pushed slowly into her.

She gasped, but did not resist his penetration. He leaned down and kissed her neck as he continued to push deeper inside her. His pet felt tight, delightfully so, but not tense.

"Master…" she whispered, wrapping her arms around him. "I love you."

His heartbeat sped up hearing those emotion-filled words. Having already made his decision, he was able to respond without hesitation. "Feel your Master's love," Ryce commanded as he began stroking her with his cock.

She purred, tears filling her eyes, "You are a part of me."

He kissed her tears while rolling his hips so that the head of his cock would rub against the place his finger had just been. He made slow, tender love to her, taking his time to enjoy the intimate moment. Ryce had forgotten what it felt like to make love to a woman. The ache in his heart matched the ache in his loins, both building to addictively extreme levels.

"You're perfect," he whispered into her ear. He continued the slow thrusts, concentrating on that one spot, needing her to come before he did.

She gasped as her muscles tensed. "I want to feel your pleasure, pet," he growled. She looked into his eyes as she came. He felt the contractions of her orgasm around his shaft and had to stay his impulse to join her until her body relaxed.

He immediately pulled out and stroked his cock vigorously. His seed shot onto her stomach in satisfying bursts. Ryce leaned over and kissed her again, stating, "Now you are mine."

"Yours forever," she said, grabbing his face in her hands and kissing him all over his cheeks, eyelids, and nose. It was a youthful thing to do and he found it charming.

He chuckled and kissed her nose, before withdrawing to clean her up. He never came inside a woman, it was his cardinal rule—one he hadn't broken since Jovita's death.

"I never thought it could be like that," she murmured as he wiped the last of it from her stomach.

He stopped what he was doing and looked at her. "You should never have known anything else."

She wrapped her arms around his thigh and purred. "As long as I am yours, it will always be good."

He petted her short, but growing, red hair. "I have so much more to show you, pet."

She looked up at him lovingly. "I cannot wait, Master." She kissed his thigh and squeezed tightly.

"But for now, I need you to finish that laundry."

She got up from the bed and gracefully redressed with a sweet smile on her face. He followed her out and brushed his horse while he watched her finish the chores. "I think we can make this work, old man."

The horse stomped his foot restlessly.

Ryce slapped his haunch. "I'm quite content, no need to sully the moment."

He should have known better. Contentment always came at a price.

It had been over a month after the accident. He had returned to hunting just as a herd of deer found refuge nearby. It meant for easy pickings and plenty of meat for his pet and Kegan's brood. What seemed a golden opportunity ended up attracting a wolf.

His pet was gathering eggs from the chickens while he butchered the young stag he'd caught earlier that day. Without warning a pack of hounds broke through the trees followed by Sir Ryan, Baron of Rannoch, and his guard. She was caught in the middle of the yard with a basket of eggs. She froze as the dogs bounded around her.

Sir Ryan called them off. "Well, well, what have we here?"

Ryce felt the hairs on the back of his neck rise. His instincts told him this would not end well, but he kept a calm voice. "Bow before the Baron, pet."

He quickly walked over to her as the Baron dismounted, speaking in perfect English, in order to impress. "Explain her presence here."

Ryce nodded to him and then gestured to his pet. "This is simply my pet, Sir Ryan, Baron of Rannoch."

The Baron licked his lips as he looked her over like a piece of meat. "A pet, you say?"

Ryce answered dryly, "Yes."

"You wouldn't be living with an unmarried Scot, would you?" he asked sarcastically.

"She is under my charge."

The Baron threw his head back and let out a high-pitched, grating laugh. "Under your charge, you say? Well, she will be under my charge tonight."

Fury burned in Ryce's chest. Had the Baron not had a guard of fifteen he would have killed him on the spot. As it was, he maintained his cool to retain control of the impetuous man. "She is my pet," he stated forcibly.

"I see…" The Baron stroked his chin as if giving the situation thought. "I am open to engaging the girl in your presence."

"That is not an option," Ryce replied.

The Baron chortled. "You have two choices, Ryce Leon. Either I return tonight to sample your pet, or I take her with me now." The guards advanced on him as if on cue.

Ryce maintained his composure, but underneath he was seething with rage. "She is under my protection," he repeated.

"I'm a reasonable man. Since I respect Saxons, let me sweeten the pot. I shall sample your pet, and in exchange I will have my priest marry you two in the morning."

Still trying to dissuade him, Ryce stated, "She is not untried, not to your tastes."

Sir Ryan raised his eyebrow, laughing unkindly. "I suspected as such, but she's so young she'll still be tight." The Baron stared at Ryce's pet as if having second thoughts. He commanded, "Look at me, girl."

She continued to look at the ground. Ryce noticed the agitation on the Baron's face as the vein in his neck pulsed rapidly. "Pet, look at the Baron," he commanded quietly.

She immediately looked up with those mesmerizing moss-colored eyes and Sir Ryan stuttered. "She's…" He cleared his throat. "The girl will do."

Ryce had to hide his disappointment. *Curse those green eyes.*

Baron shook his head. "Trying to keep her a secret wasn't shrewd, Leon. We Scots don't appreciate our girls being sullied by the likes of you. Yes, it would be prudent to make it a legitimate union. However, if you'd rather, I shall take her off your hands and use her as I please."

Ryce bristled at his implied threat, not trusting himself to speak.

The Baron glanced back to her. "You would prefer to be married, girl. Is that not correct?"

She looked down at the ground again. "If it pleases my Master."

The Baron looked at Ryce incredulously. "Master?" Then he chuckled under his breath. "It is obvious she wants what is due her. Make her a proper bride, Leon, and avoid the unpleasantries."

The logical side of Ryce's brain kicked in. If he could not annihilate the threat, then being present at her taking would give him control over what happened to his pet... to Chrisselle. Yes, he was calling her by her given name again. Fate seemed to demand it.

Ryce was not anxious to marry the girl, but if it would protect her from this piss of a man it was an acceptable cost. It would also free him from having to hide her indefinitely. But, God's teeth, the price...

The Baron slapped his crop against his hand in agitation. "This isn't a hard choice. Either invite me to her bed tonight or I take her from you now."

Ryce looked at him with contempt. "You are invited to return."

The Baron nodded with a superior smile and turned back to Chrisselle. "Girl, it appears your master wants to share. Don't disappoint." He mounted his horse and dug his heels into the white stallion. "I'm off to hunt." The hounds were given the signal and bounded off howling towards the unlucky herd. Ryce was certain there would be no deer left after the Baron was done 'hunting'.

Ryce looked at Chrisselle and saw that the basket in her hand was shaking. "Put down the eggs and come to me," he said tenderly.

She laid down the basket on the ground and rushed into his open arms. Ryce held her tightly, understanding what a difficult task was ahead. He did not want Chrisselle to be damaged by the Baron. She had already been used once and there would be terrible consequences if she was taken against her will again.

The key lay in how he presented it to her. If he was able to provide her with a sense of control and the assurance of safety, this unwelcomed event would not have to define Chrisselle. He lifted her chin and looked into those green eyes that had betrayed her. "Do you wish to marry me?"

She nodded, her eyes conveying joy at the prospect. *Good.*

"I concur. I think you will make a fine wife."

She smiled, her eyes glowing with love.

And now to set up the scene to get her through it. "Although the Baron's invitation was unexpected,"—he felt her tense—"I find it intriguing. It would please me to see you with another man."

She searched his eyes. He knew she did not care for the Baron, but the submissive in her wanted to please her Master. He would need to use her desire to please him. He would help Chrisselle approach it as a learning opportunity.

"There is much I can discover as I watch you with another man. It allows me to observe your body's responses to different stimuli. He may please you in ways that I have yet to learn."

He saw her short, rapid breaths and knew she was frightened by the prospect. "As your Master, I will always protect you. You are my first and only concern. I would not agree to this if I thought you would be harmed."

She took a deep breath and smiled up at him. "Thank you, Master."

It was imperative that she see it as an opportunity, not something forced on her. "I am grateful the Baron's visit will end our need for secrecy. It will please me to show you off to the community."

Her smile grew wider. "I would like that very much, Master."

Ryce stroked her cheek with his calloused thumb. "No one is as beautiful as my Scottish pet, no wonder the Baron is enchanted by you. I believe marriage is the only way to discourage others from stealing you from me."

Her cheeks became rosy, and she looked down at her feet.

He lifted her chin and smiled with restrained confidence. "Tonight we play, tomorrow we wed, future wife."

"My future husband…" Chrisselle blushed again, suddenly becoming shy.

"Go put the eggs away," he told her with a light tone. He watched her skip over to pick them up and she headed to the cottage.

He would have to use his skills to read the Baron tonight as much as Chrisselle. It was going to be a difficult balance, but he was determined to bring her through it unscathed.

Sharing His Pet

S ir Ryan, the Baron of Rannoch, arrived as the sun was just disappearing behind the horizon. He had his large entourage with him, anticipating Ryce would not be a willing participant in this unwelcomed exchange. "Is your pet ready to please her Baron?"

"*We* are looking forward to tonight's events," Ryce replied.

The Baron's high-pitched laughter filled the night air. "I hope you understand you are only there to observe."

"I will not interfere, Baron, but I do intend to enhance the experience."

The Baron looked at his guards with an amused expression. "If he lays a hand on me, be prepared to cut it off."

There was uncomfortable laughter from his men. The group dismounted and five guards followed them into the cottage. Chrisselle was kneeling on the ground naked, collared and chained, with her head bowed.

"You really do treat her like a pet. How odd, Leon."

Ryce said nothing as the men lined the walls of the room. He could sense Chrisselle's tension rise, but he had warned her that she would be watched by the guards. There was no way the Baron would leave Ryce alone with him. Sir Ryan was a fool, but he had no death wish.

"She only follows my commands."

"How convenient," the Baron snorted.

"But she follows them impeccably," Ryce added.

The Baron raised his eyebrow. "Does she now?"

"What is your pleasure?"

Sir Ryan looked at her hungrily. "I would like to see her talents."

"Pet, undress the Baron and pleasure him with your mouth."

Chrisselle obediently rocked onto her heels and stood gracefully. Ryce heard the intake of breath from some of the men. Her body had filled out enough to be womanly, but she maintained an innocent appearance.

She walked over to the Baron and slowly began the laborious task of removing his many layers of clothing. It was obvious that the Baron was a lover of fashion, something that Ryce had no patience for.

Naked, the Baron appeared soft and fleshy. More noticeable, however, was the small example of manhood between his legs. *No wonder he prefers virgins,* Ryce thought. But he saw it as a welcome surprise. Such a minuscule shaft would prove easier for Chrisselle to take.

She gracefully knelt again and grasped the minute cock in her hands and took him into her mouth. The Baron grabbed onto a nearby chair for support as she flicked her tongue up and down his shaft, lightly sucking his balls and teething his cock.

She pulled away and looked up at the Baron. "Don't stop, girl," he barked.

She instinctively glanced at Ryce, who nodded. Chrisselle continued her passionate oral pleasures to the grunts and groans of the Baron. At one point, he fisted her short hair and pumped his cock into her mouth.

Ryce tensed, not sure if Chrisselle could handle such rough treatment. To her credit, she took his shaft deeper into her mouth and even moaned for his enjoyment. The Baron instantly pulled out. "No, not yet. I do not want my shaft spent so easily."

His confession was music to Ryce's ears. Knowing the Baron was already on the edge would make it easy to orchestrate a quick session.

"Would you like her to escort you to the bed, Baron?"

The man's cheeks were flushed. It was obvious that the man was struggling to keep his composure. "Aye, that would do."

Chrisselle stood up and took his hand, moving with cat-like elegance as she led him to the bed. The girl was truly a gem among women.

Ryce followed them to the bed, taking off his shirt in the process. He stood at the head of the bed and asked her to lie down on her back. He took her wrists and pulled them over her head, accentuating her lovely breasts.

"Exquisite," the Baron said, licking his lips.

"Yes, and she enjoys being played with."

Sir Ryan took that as his cue and lay down by her side, grabbing her breasts like an overeager boy. His wet lips encased one of her pink nipples and he began sucking and tugging on her nipples. She tilted her head back and looked Ryce in the eyes as he held her wrists above her head. "That's it, pet. Enjoy the Baron's lovemaking." Inside, however, he was growling. The man had no finesse at all.

Tonight was going to be like training two instead of one. To Sir Ryan he stated, "I find that my pet becomes more wet when a tongue is flicked across her nipple."

The Baron grunted in irritation, but his hand disappeared between her legs to sample her moistness as he changed tactics with his tongue. Chrisselle responded by mewing softly. A sound that Ryce's shaft instantly responded to. It ached to plunge inside her feminine depths.

"The girl is ready," Sir Ryan announced as he changed position. His tiny shaft poked out between his legs, pulsing and rigid. Ryce couldn't believe he was moving so quickly and had misgivings.

The Baron spread Chrisselle's legs apart to examine her mound critically. "Definitely used and abused goods."

Ryce felt Chrisselle tense in shame. He responded with a smooth, commanding voice. "What you have before you is the beauty of womanhood, Baron of Rannoch. I doubt you have seen any more lovely than my pet. Pink, swollen, inviting petals that call a man's cock to partake of her heaven."

He noticed that the Baron's shaft pulsed as he reexamined Chrisselle and a drop of precome oozed from the tip of his cock. The man spread her legs wider, preparing to thrust, but Ryce place his hand over Chrisselle's mound, blocking it from the assault.

"What's the meaning of this?" Sir Ryan demanded.

The tension of all the guards permeated the room.

Ryce continued to keep his calm demeanor. "Enter my pet slowly, Baron. Appreciate the tightness of her tunnel, the moistness of her excitement for you. To plow right in is to miss the invitation of her lust."

Sir Ryan shook his head. "You speak flowery words, Leon."

"I speak the truth. Smell her, are you not affected by her moist odor?" Ryce removed his hand.

The Baron leaned forward and took a whiff. "Aye, it does excite. But I need no more prodding. I am about to explode," he complained.

"Have your way with her then... slowly. You will find she is as tight as any virgin." Ryce ran his hands up her arms seductively and secured Chrisselle's wrists in his hands again. "I would like to hold her down while I watch you partake of her."

"You English are a sick lot," he chuckled.

He positioned his small cock against her wet hole and, taking Ryce's advice, slowly disappeared into her pussy. It was not pleasant to watch, but Ryce kept his face relaxed. He noticed that Chrisselle was observing him intently, wanting to know if she was pleasing her Master or not.

He smiled down at her, leaning over to give her a fiery kiss. 'Isn't it agreeable, pet, to feel the passion of two men?"

The Baron's face was already red and sweating. It was obvious he was struggling not to climax too soon. Ryce chuckled to himself, knowing exactly what needed to be done.

"Arch your back, pet. Give the Baron all of you."

She did so without hesitation. Sir Ryan groaned, the feel of it too much for his cock to take, and he immediately pumped his seed into her, grunting like an animal. He pulled out afterwards, looking a bit chagrined.

"I told you she was like no other," Ryce said, smiling. He stared at the now miniature shaft between the Baron's legs. The man looked down, then got off the bed and hurriedly dressed in his undergarments.

Ryce said casually, "I can tell you have excited my pet to an unusual level."

The Baron looked up, seemingly surprised and intrigued. Ryce wondered how many girls he had ruined with his sexless pounding. Ryce felt it his duty to show the blaggard ways of pleasuring a woman.

"Would you mind if I stoke the fires further?"

Sir Ryan instantly warned him, "You are not allowed to take her."

Ryce understood his tactics. He wanted to ensure his pathetic seed would have a chance to impregnate Chrisselle. "Of course, Baron. However, my pet needs attending to after your lively session." It was laughable, but the Baron bought it.

"You have my permission."

Ryce lowered himself onto the bed and kissed his pet as his hand traveled down between her legs. He slipped his middle finger into her and swirled around Chrisselle's wet walls while he sucked on her erect nipples. He pulled his finger out and discreetly wiped the Baron's viscous fluid onto the blanket before diving back into her responsive depths repeatedly. Chrisselle did not suspect his true intentions and lifted her hips in eager acceptance of his touch each time he reentered her with his fingers. It helped bring validity to his deception as Sir Ryan watched in rapt attention.

When he felt the hated seed was out, he began concentrating on bringing her to climax. "Open your legs, pet. Let the Baron see the fruits of his labor."

She spread her legs wide open, baring her sex for all to see. Ryce turned her head towards him and kissed her deeply as he stroked her to climax. Her body arched and she moaned in his mouth as she came for him. Ryce groaned in response, wanting her to know his pleasure.

He did not pull away until the last of her contractions ended. Then he looked to the Baron. "I told you she was provoked by your attention."

Sir Ryan puffed out his chest. "I find they are all gluttonous whores for powerful men."

Ryce shook his head. "I know my pet. I think it had to do more with the way you handled her tonight." He hoped by praising the Baron's more gentle way of taking her, he might change the man's tactics in the future to pleasuring women instead of scarring them.

Sir Ryan ate up the commendation. "You may have trouble with her now, knowing she is thinking of me when you bed her."

It was a struggle not to laugh in his face. "I am sure that was part of your intent."

"It is an unfortunate effect," he sniffed conceitedly. "Have your pet dress me now."

Ryce looked at Chrisselle tenderly. "Do as the Baron wishes."

She got up from the bed and sensually redressed the Baron. Ryce could tell she was doing it for his own benefit—her attempt to entice her Master even as she attended to another. *I will be taking you, pet*, he thought as he watched her graceful movements.

Thankfully, the Baron left shortly after, looking drained from his long day of hunting and recent orgasm. Before he left, however, he announced. "My priest will be over at first light to marry you. No more hiding, Ryce Leon. Oh, and the collar must go. I do not want rumors to spread about you."

Chrisselle instinctively clasped her collar in defense, but remained respectfully silent.

"As you wish," Ryce answered.

"That's a good man. I will expect adequate compensation for the favor I have bestowed on you." He whipped his horse around and galloped off with his fifteen men and countless deer carcasses in tow.

Ryce could not hide his contempt, and snorted in anger. The man was a stain upon his own people. Unworthy of being in charge. He returned to the cottage and called Chrisselle to him. "My beauty, I am well pleased." She smiled at him, a look of pure adoration. It warmed his heart to know he had succeeded in keeping her safe and intact. However, there was still one more thing he needed to do before the night was over.

"I will set the water over the fire. You will cleanse yourself before I receive you as my wife. I do not see the necessity of waiting until the morning."

The look of love she gave him was disarming. The girl really did have an uncommon pull on his heart—one he had not allowed himself to experience in a long, long time. It was both invigorating and alarming. With great love came great loss. It was inevitable.

He sat back and watched her bathe, enjoying the look of her smooth skin, the pertness of her young breasts, and the delicate curve of her long neck. It was markedly different from the first time she had bathed in the washtub, clutching her chest with her crazy hair poking every which way. It astounded him how much had changed between them, despite his best efforts to keep her at bay, and now he was getting married to her.

Life never ceased to amaze him, even after many lifespans.

He dried her off when she was done and carried her to the bed, laying Chrisselle down gently. "Now it is my turn to claim my wife. No other man will touch you after this. I will not allow it."

She beamed.

"To mark this new beginning, there is something I must do." He opened her legs, putting the soles of her feet together so that she was spread wide. He did not explain as he dipped his hands in the tepid bath water and lathered his hands. He returned to her and covered her mound with the suds, then he retrieved his knife and began the delicate work of shaving her. It took an exorbitant amount of time, but he was in no hurry. The ritual was necessary.

Chrisselle gasped as the blade scraped across her sensitive skin, but she did not twitch. When he was finished, he rinsed her off and dried her bare mound. He touched it reverently. "Tonight marks our beginning as husband and wife. What happened in the past is no longer. This is about me taking you as my virginal bride… whole and untouched."

She blinked away the tears in her eyes as she nodded in understanding. He lay down beside her and traced her feminine curves with his fingers. He truly saw her as his untouched bride, caressing her skin with sensual wonderment. It was soft, smooth and virginal in its white color. The rosy pink of her nipples spoke of her innocence, and her naked womanhood of her youth.

"You are beautiful, Chrisselle, my pet," he whispered.

She looked at him with renewed devotion. The power of her given name was something Ryce understood well. She would forever remain his pet, but as wife she would become so much more.

He lightly grazed her pink lips and watched her shudder from the ticklish feel of it. "Kiss me, wife."

She leaned forward, pressing her breasts against him as she complied with his command. Her kiss was tentative and tender. He pressed her closer and she responded by darting her tongue in his mouth. He growled under his breath, wanting to encourage her lustful nature. He was taking a virgin, yes, but he desired a responsive and passionate woman.

"Everything about you is perfect," he murmured, as he played with her red locks. "Your hair is like the sun, and your eyes… a place I long to get lost into." He kissed each eyelid.

Ryce lightly touched her erect nipples, teasing them. "Their roseate color invites the attention of my tongue." He leaned over and gently bit her left nipple before sucking on it and he was rewarded with her gasp.

It was an invitation to feel between her legs. Of course, she was moist with need. Ryce kissed her flat stomach, caressing her thighs, building up the anticipation of his tongue on her bare mound. He commented, "You are filling out to be a curvaceous woman." He trailed his hands over her hips. "I can't help but want to take you every time you bend over. That shapely ass calls to my cock. I find laundry day especially tempting."

She giggled. "I never knew, Master."

"I am a man of discipline," he growled into her ear.

Ryce gazed at her mound, admiring its naked look. "My pet, your womanhood is pure perfection in taste and appearance." He settled down between her legs. Her mound was the color of a blushing rose glistening with dew. Ryce took a long lick of it.

gift cards.

Díganos acerca de su visita a Walmart hoy y usted podría ganar una de las 5 tarjetas de regalo de Walmart de $1000 o una de las 750 tarjetas de regalo de Walmart de $100.

http://www.survey.walmart.com

No purchase necessary. Must be 18 or older and a legal resident of the 50 US, DC, or PR to enter. To enter without purchase and for official rules, visit www.entry.survey.walmart.com.

Sweepstakes period ends on the date outlined in the official rules. Survey must be taken within ONE week of today. Void where prohibited.

Walmart

770-554-7481 Mgr: JOHN
4221 ATLANTA HWY
LOGANVILLE GA 30052

ST# 05252 OP# 009039 TE# 39 TR# 00783

GV YOGURT	007874210061 F	3.62 V
RAMEN-BEEF	004178900014 F	0.37 V
RAMEN-BEEF	004178900142 F	0.37 V
HF BK FST HM	004450032953 F	3.28 V
CANISTER PO	007874223707 F	1.00 R
PIZZA	087282400981 F	0.80 V
PIZZA	087282400981 F	0.80 V
CANISTER PO	007874223708 F	1.00 R
GV .5L WATER	007874227909 F	3.98 R

DISCOUNT GIVEN   0.60

SUBTOTAL   1.62

TAX 2

She responded by mewing, which caused his cock to stiffen further. Her lips were swollen with her lust, beckoning him to partake of her depths.

He concentrated on her erect nodule, pulling back the hood to lavish his attention on it. She bucked her hips at the intensity of the stimulation, so he held her down and whispered, "Relax."

Chrisselle lay back on the bed, and he felt the tension of her muscles ease. She was such an obedient pet. He flicked his tongue against her smooth pearl, noting the jolts of sensation he incited by her uncontrolled twitching. It was entertaining, but his desire for her was causing an uncomfortable ache in his groin.

He crawled up between her legs and kissed her lips as the head of his cock pressed against her wet opening. "Time to accept me as your husband."

She wrapped her arms around him. "It is my honor."

Ryce pushed into her hot sex slowly, as if he was taking her as his virginal bride. This was not about using her for his pleasure, this was a connection of souls, a physical representation of their commitment. "You are fully pleasing to me, wife," he said as he pushed into her depths. She was tight and moist, encompassing the entire length of his shaft.

Her breath was quick, her arousal easy to discern, but it was love that shone in her eyes.

Ryce began stroking her firm walls with his cock. "You are mine."

The two moved as one as they made love to one another. It was tender, emotional, and hot as Hades. Ryce looked into her moss-colored eyes as he allowed himself to come inside her after decades of denying himself the pleasure. His balls contracted as the powerful release of his seed burst forth.

Chrisselle cried out as if she could feel the heat of it.

His cock pumped load after load deep inside his bride, overwhelming what remained of the Baron's seed. Ryce's entire body shuddered from the monumental release, from his shoulders down to his toes. He groaned loudly from the strength of it. Afterwards, he slowly pulled out and collapsed on her.

It took him a moment to realize she was crying. He brushed away the tears with his thumb. "What is wrong, pet?"

"Master... husband, you are inside me." She ran her hands over her pelvis lovingly as if she could feel his seed within her.

"Yes, my pet," he said, kissing her on the lips. "Consider yourself claimed."

She smiled. "I am yours forever, Master."

"Aye."

He lay beside her and stared up at the roof of his cottage. He'd broken his cardinal rule not to release his seed inside a woman, but tonight had been a unique circumstance. Ryce could not allow that piss of a man to father a child, even if that meant the unwelcomed chance of fathering one of his own.

Ryce stared into her radiant eyes. "I love you for more than your beautiful face, pleasing body, and obedient heart." He lightly caressed the side of her face. "Your strong spirit astounds me. Having been through so much in your young life, you still possess a positive temperament and have not let the wrongs of the past define you."

"Master…"

He put his fingers to her lips. "You may call me by my given name tonight, Chrisselle."

She blushed as she pronounced his name for the first time. "Ryce… I have always known I was destined to find a powerful man like my father. Waiting for you helped me during the black days."

His laughter was a low, sweet rumble as he recalled how frightened and emaciated she had been when he first encountered her. "You did not appear to know your Master when we met that first day, my tiny waif."

"I was blind… Ryce. I was going to run that night. You were not part of the plan."

"But you wouldn't have made it far in your condition," he stated somberly.

"What did it matter? I would have died free."

Ryce nodded in understanding. "Yes, there is great worth in freedom." He looked at her gravely. "You have the courage of a lion, Chrisselle. Worthy of the name Leon."

She broke into an enchanting smile. "Thank you."

"Are you ready to be my wife?"

"I have been since the day you hand-fed me back to health. I knew then I would deny you nothing."

"Why is that, Chrisselle?"

"You are my destiny."

He felt a soul-shiver. It was disconcerting to think there was such a thing as fate, for if that was the case his future was decided—a reality he could not accept. Yet looking into the depth of her eyes he felt at peace, as if everything had lined up to create this moment in time.

Chrisselle

The elderly priest came early the next day, wanting to get the inconvenient task behind him. Chrisselle stayed in the cottage to ready herself. She had dressed in her only remaining tartan, the lovely green having been bloodied during his accident months ago. However, she wore the red tartan proudly and had taken great care with her hair. *She needn't have bothered*, he thought. The glow in her eyes was all Ryce needed.

He wore his formal kilt of a similar pattern and strapped his impressive claymore on his back, in full Highland dress including jacket, dirk and sporran for the occasion. Chrisselle stood back to admire him. "Master, you are frighteningly handsome."

He smiled at her roguishly. "Thank you, my pet." Ryce motioned her to him. His hands unbuckled the leather collar around her neck. She gasped and whispered, "No…"

"As per the Baron's request," he replied, tucking it in the waist of his kilt.

He bent over and picked a sprig of white heather growing beside the cottage and tucked it behind her ear. "Now you are ready."

A sweet flush colored her face. "Thank you, Master… Leon."

"We are set to proceed," Ryce announced to the priest, handing him a braided cord of red and white. "We have no rings."

Ryce clasped Chrisselle's hand and the withered old man bound them together. "May God be with you and bless you. May you see your children's children. May you be poor in misfortune, rich in blessings. May you know nothing but happiness from this day forward." The priest nodded to Ryce.

He looked down at his youthful bride. "I, Ryce Garrett Leon, now take you, Chrisselle Buchanan, to be my wife. In the presence of God and before this witness, I promise to be a loving, faithful and loyal husband to you, until God shall separate us by death."

She gazed up into his eyes, radiant with joy. "I, Chrisselle Buchanan, now take you, Ryce Garrett Leon, to be my husband. In the presence of God and before this witness I promise to be a loving, faithful and loyal wife to you, until God shall separate us by death."

The ancient man waddled to their cottage and began blessing it, while Ryce untied the cord. He asked her to turn around, placing it around her delicate neck and tying it so that it was comfortably snug against her throat. He leaned over and whispered, "Now we won't draw attention to ourselves."

She twisted around and kissed him on the lips.

He tasted the saltiness of her tears. "Why the tears?"

"My heart wants to burst with happiness."

He chuckled and picked her up, carrying his bride over the threshold of his home as was tradition, just in time to see the priest blessing the marriage bed. Ryce put her down gently, kissing Chrisselle on the forehead.

The old man shuffled over to them when he was done. He held out his hand and Ryce quickly pressed coins into it. "Thank you, Father."

The withered figure bowed slightly and left their home without another word.

Ryce smiled at his pet, now wife. "You are lawfully Chrisselle Ryce Leon."

She gracefully bowed at his feet. "I am honored, Lord."

"No, Chrisselle, never lord, only Master."

"Yes, Master."

"Today, I want you to call me Ryce."

Her eyes grew wide and she blushed deeply. Her submissive nature made it a challenge for her and it pleased him.

"It is my intention to introduce you to the community today. I do not want rumors or doubts surrounding our unexpected union. It is very important to me."

"Yes, that would be verra nice," she said eagerly.

He suspected she was anxious to connect with others. His carnal needs could wait until they returned from their outing. "I will saddle Eventide and we will head out." Ryce walked to the barn to the nickering welcome of his friend.

He got out the metal comb and began brushing the thick midnight mane, desiring that they all make an impression that day. While he worked the knots out, he joked with his steed. "Yes, I have made my life as complicated as possible. I think you suspected it from the beginning." Ryce slapped his muscular shoulder good-naturedly. "Still… she makes a fine partner."

He started on the tail. Eventide lifted his foot threateningly when Ryce tried to brush through a particularly difficult knot of hair and twigs. "Don't even think of it," he warned. "If you weren't so careless where you walked, you wouldn't have weeds in your tail."

The horse threw back his head several times in complaint, but his hoof remained on the ground. Once Eventide was thoroughly combed, Ryce cinched the saddle and stood back to admire his work. Eventide was an impressive beast, with his toned equine flesh, dark grey coat and long black mane and tail. However, it was his intelligence and fearless spirit that made the animal truly remarkable.

Ryce went to the chest in the back of the barn and retrieved some coins for the day's festivities before calling Chrisselle to join him. He smirked when she weaved heather in Eventide's mane.

"Ah, you look properly domestic," Ryce informed his stallion.

Eventide rubbed his cheek against Chrisselle in a gesture of acceptance. It appeared his steed didn't mind looking 'pretty' for her sake. Ryce whispered into his closest velvet ear, "She seems to have you under the same spell. Welcome to the club, old man."

Ryce helped Chrisselle onto Eventide and climbed up behind her. It was a pleasant morning with the crisp Highland air and clear skies. He wrapped one arm around her waist and guided the reins with the other. Chrisselle trembled in his arms, excited at the prospect of meeting others.

He headed to Avril's. Ryce wanted her to be the first to know. He held the woman in high esteem and did not want her to hear it from another. Ryce also trusted that her open spirit would allow her to accept the new situation between he and Chrisselle.

Avril was more than a little surprised to discover that he was recently married and that Chrisselle was the woman she had sewn the dresses for. Luckily, his young bride's enthusiasm for Avril's seamstress skills disarmed her reservations.

Avril shared with Chrisselle her love of her craft and the two were soon talking like sisters as she demonstrated the process. Ryce leaned against the door and listened to them with amusement. Eventually, their conversations moved on to more serious topics as the two shared their difficult childhoods. Ryce had to cut it short when they began discussing his influence on them, not enjoying the sense of discomfort their praises wrought.

"We have many households to visit today and must be going."

Avril appeared distraught when they readied to leave. "Please come visit soon, Avril," Chrisselle begged.

Avril glanced at Ryce to see his reaction. He nodded and replied, "You would be welcomed."

"It would be grand for Master Leon and I to entertain you," Chrisselle added.

Ryce wondered if his new bride understood the image her words conjured up. He shifted himself on the saddle so it wouldn't be so readily apparent. He turned Eventide towards the MacPherson farm next.

It appeared that the Baron had already informed the MacPhersons of the nuptials, and because of that word had spread quickly. At every house, Ryce made sure to throw coins to the children in accordance with an old wedding tradition. It helped to soften the villagers' sentiments concerning their oddly secretive marriage. However, it was Chrisselle's endearing personality that won people's hearts over.

Near the end of the day, his pet was chattering on and on about the different families she'd met. Everyone had been hospitable to them except Kegan, their last stop.

His temporary sex slave had taken the news hard, giving them a chilly reception. She was not pleased when Ryce tossed coins to her eager brood. He refused to deal with her jealousy, and thanked her for keeping silent about Chrisselle before abruptly leaving.

On his way out, Kegan said, "I care nothing for her; however, I still crave time with you." Then she added in an intimate whisper, "I will *always* be available for you… Master."

He reminded her coolly, "Your treatment of my wife determines our future relationship."

She shrugged her shoulders. "Then I suppose we have none, *Lord* Leon." Kegan swished her attractive ass as she turned away and sauntered back to her offspring.

Ryce shook his head. Did she really think her feminine wiles would make up for her brazen lack of respect?

He looked skyward and saw dark ominous clouds swirling above them. "Come, wife, we must return home." He pushed Eventide, but they were soon pelted by cold raindrops whipping about in the fierce winds. What made it far worse was the intense lightning and thunder. A lesser horse would have panicked and dumped his riders when a strike hit close by, but his stallion ignored his own welfare. By the time they made it safely to the barn, all three were chilled to the bone.

Ryce commanded Chrisselle to go and start a fire before undressing completely. He took care of Eventide, drying off his courageous steed. "I can always rely on you, old friend. Too bad I can't invite you in to sit by the fire and share some spirits with me."

Eventide snorted and hit Ryce in the gut playfully.

"I suppose an extra helping of feed is more appreciated." He laid a blanket over the stallion's back and left a generous portion of food. He ran to the cottage amidst crashing thunder and pelting rain. When he slammed the door behind him, he found a large fire roaring pleasantly and Chrisselle kneeling beside the bed, naked except for the cord around her neck. It was a stunning sight.

The new collar suited her, simple in its beauty and profound in its symbolism. Her fiery hair had grown out to her shoulders and framed her face beautifully. As far as her body, it was fully pleasing. Her pert breasts were a delectable, indulgent handful, her round ass an erotic poem, and her bare mound a seductive siren's song to his cock.

He undressed where he was, leaving his clothes dripping over a chair, before walking over to the bed and sitting next to his pet. The wind howled angrily outside and the rain pounded the cottage relentlessly. The power of the storm added to Ryce's libido.

"Pleasure your husband."

Chrisselle looked up at him with those green jewels and smiled. She moved between his legs and took hold of his rigid shaft. "My handsome Master Ryce," she purred as her lips caressed his cool but throbbing cock. Her warm tongue played with the ridge of his foreskin and she mewed when she tasted the drop of his essence caused by her attention.

Ryce stroked her red locks as she continued and then grasped the back of her head and guided her to take more of his manhood. She eagerly complied, taking him deeply. After spending the day imagining coupling with her, Ryce was overly sensitive and had to pull her off.

She glanced up at him questioningly with a hint of sadness in her eyes.

"Your husband has other plans tonight."

Chrisselle's smile returned, her relief at not failing him easy to read on her face.

"I want you to straddle your mound over my face while encasing your lips around my shaft."

Her eyes widened at the prospect.

Ryce lay on the bed and motioned her to him with a seductive grin. Chrisselle giggled nervously as a large crash of thunder sounded above them. She crawled onto the bed and carefully lifted her leg over his face. He stared at her tantalizing bare sex and growled, "Come here, beautiful," grabbing both buttocks and pressing her sweet pearl to his mouth.

She cried out as he began sucking on the erect nodule, but he soon gasped when he felt the tantalizing warmth of her mouth engulf his cock. Ryce groaned in manly satisfaction. Experiencing the smell and taste of her while she sucked on his shaft was the ultimate high.

He broke his suction on her sex and commanded quietly, "Suck harder, pet."

Instantly the pressure on his shaft increased and he growled in satisfaction. Ryce applied the same amount of suction and soon had her squirming from the sexual torment. He slowly eased his thumb into her wet tunnel and felt her pelvis buck against him in response. Suddenly the tempo of her oral stimulation increased tenfold and he almost exploded in her mouth.

"Slow down, pet," he barked, trying to rein in the orgasm threatening.

Chrisselle immediately stopped the motion, but did not release the pressure. His cock pulsated inside her mouth as he concentrated on the raging storm outside to halt the impending climax.

Once he had regained control, he laid his head back and gazed at her womanhood. Her outer lips were swollen, the opening dripping with her lust and her pink puckered hole begging for his attention. It was an area he had not explored yet, and their wedding night seemed a perfect time to give her a taste of the forbidden fruit. But only a taste…

"Chrisselle, I want you to make love to your Master."

She released his cock and turned her head. "How, my husband?"

"Lie on me, I will guide my shaft into you."

She shuddered in anticipation and repositioned herself, laying her breasts against his chest. He took his shaft in one hand and held onto her waist with the other as he pressed into her moist harbor. Her passionate cry caught in her throat when he gripped her hips and thrust himself deeper.

Ryce growled lustfully as he lifted her up and then let her tight warmth settle back down onto his cock. "Look, pet. I want you to see the beauty of your sex taking my manhood."

She looked down and whimpered as her eager sex took his thick shaft down to the base. Chrisselle was captivated by the sensual vision of it.

While she watched, he ran his middle finger around the rim of her opening, covering his hand in her juices. Then he grabbed her ass and thrust his cock as deep as it would go. "Kiss me, wife."

She smiled as her lips came down on his, their tongues beginning their sexual dance. While in that intimate embrace, he felt the edges of her puckered hole.

Chrisselle tensed, but did not move. He slowly teased her arsehole. Just as he was going to penetrate her with his finger, a loud crack of thunder boomed above their heads. She cried out in surprise and fear, but it only caused to excite him further. He murmured into her ear, "Let me in, pet," as he pressed the taut opening, his finger slipping inside her untouched hole.

She was panting now, but her tongue thrust deeper into his mouth letting Ryce know her state of arousal. He pushed his finger in further, feeling the resistance of her tight muscles but gently forcing her body's compliance. "Good girl."

Ryce began pumping his cock inside her depths as he explored her virginal hole with his finger. The deeper he pushed the more she whimpered, the more her juices flowed. It was intoxicating and took him over the edge.

With his middle finger lodged deep in her ass, his cock exploded with an abundance of his seed. Thrust after powerful thrust, he filled her with himself while thunder crashed around them. They both lay panting from the intensity of the experience.

Ryce promised himself it would be the last time he would come inside her. He could ill afford the complications or the emotional toll of Chrisselle becoming pregnant. However, he convinced himself that this had been worth the risk. He hadn't felt such an intensive, awe-inspiring orgasm since… *her.*

He shook the memory of Jovita from his mind, kissing his wife's sweaty skin instead. "You are extraordinary."

She wrapped her arms around him, purring in contentment. "Everything you do feels good, Ryce. Everything."

Chrisselle fell asleep to the sounds of the violent storm raging outside, sheltered in his arms. For Ryce there was a sense of overwhelming peace—and hope.

But memories of Jovita would come back to haunt him a few days later. He had just finished feeding Eventide and was walking back to the cottage for a quick breakfast when he saw her bent over, retching in the bushes.

A cold chill coursed through his bones. *Jovita.*

She had been the same way, showing signs of the pregnancy early on. Struggling to keep food down as their child grew in her belly. It had been a difficult pregnancy. It was only towards the end that Jovita had recovered and started to glow with motherhood. He'd thought they had made it through the worst of it then, having no idea what fate had in store.

A streak of crimson flashed through his mind and he howled in rage. He had done this!

Chrisselle stood up and looked at him in fear. He could not face her or this unwanted reality. Ryce went back to the barn, not even bothering to saddle Eventide. He fastened the reins, jumped on his back and galloped away from her and his mistake.

Ryce eventually ended up at Avril's and it was she who helped Ryce think beyond his past. "I hae always wanted a wee bairn, Master Leon! Wull ye let me visit often once the babe is born?"

Her overwhelming enthusiasm made his fears seem unfounded. Chrisselle's pregnancy would not end in tragedy like Jovita's. The situations were nothing alike. This community had accepted them both into the fold. Surely these people would not be so quick to turn if they uncovered his secret. Chrisselle would not be punished, as Jovita had been, for carrying the child of a devil.

"Yes, Avril. I am sure Chrisselle would appreciate your company. In fact, she's mentioned several times that she would enjoy a visit from you."

"It wull be ma pleasure, Master Leon." Avril added shyly, "Ah wull make another dress for her to replace the ane that wus lost." Ryce had not explained why Chrisselle was missing a dress; the fewer people who knew of his accident the better.

"May I request that you make another green one? It brings out the color of her eyes."

Avril blushed and turned away. "Ma pleasure, Master Leon," she said quietly.

Ryce wondered if she was struggling with her own jealousy. If she was, he gave Avril credit for keeping it in check. He handed over several coins.

She refused to take them. "Oh nah, tae much."

He laughed gently. "It is payment for a dress for Chrisselle and one for yourself. I would like to see you in something new."

The flush on Avril's face was lovely to see. "Ah cannae…" she sputtered.

Ryce put his fingers to her lips. "It is my desire."

Tears came to her eyes. He brushed her scarred cheek lightly. "Treat yourself well, Avril. I command it."

She smiled. "Aye, Ah wull, Master Leon."

"And come visit us soon."

He left with a much lighter spirit and was pleased to see Chrisselle looking better when he returned. She met him in the barn and asked hesitantly, "Master?"

Ryce held out his arms and she raced to them. "It is fine, pet. Ghosts from my past… they do not concern you."

She pressed her head against his chest. "I thought I had displeased my husband."

He lifted her chin. "No. I find you fully pleasing." He kissed her roughly, releasing his longing and fear in the connection. Afterwards, he felt cleansed of his misgivings. "I love you, pet."

She squeezed him tight. "I love you, Master."

He chose to be upfront with her. "I visited Avril today because I believe you to be pregnant."

Chrisselle gasped and asked in a breathless whisper, "Truly?"

"Yes, my wife. Avril will come by in a few days to check on you."

She rubbed her stomach reverently. "A babe so soon?"

Ryce threw out the momentary doubt that it was his. "I am a virile man, pet. It is the reason I normally spill my seed."

Chrisselle blushed and giggled. "I did feel its power, Master."

"I do have a powerful cock," he stated smugly, winking at her. But then he became serious. "Chrisselle, you must take it easy until the sickness passes. I want nothing to happen to you or the child."

She beamed at him. "*Our* child."

He let his defenses down then, embracing her and this chance at new life. "Aye, my Scottish pet, our child."

Wicked, Wicked Fate

F|ate was not kind.

Near the end of Chrisselle's pregnancy, Ryce woke with a start to urgent pounding on the door. So urgent, in fact, that he jumped out of bed and stumbled in the darkness to open it while still in the nude. Avril stood in his doorway, panting for breath. She stared at him, seemingly unaware of his lack of dress as she gasped out her message.

"Men... comin'... fur ye!"

He grabbed her arm and pulled her inside. Chrisselle came to him and handed Ryce his kilt. He quickly dressed, asking Avril questions in the process. "Who is coming? What do you mean they are coming for me?"

"Band o' rebels... comin' for the Sassenach."

He grabbed her shoulders. "Who is coming for the Saxon?"

"The Gregor clan. Comin' tae kull the Baron of Rannoch, but gaun tae get rid o' his Sassenach pet first."

"How far?"

"Verra close!"

"Quick, take Chrisselle with you." He left the cottage, commanding that they follow. Ryce headed straight for the barn. He unlocked the chest and rifled through it, taking only a handful of coins from a heavy leather bag before handing it to Chrisselle. "Take this, but hide it when you get to Avril's. No one must know you have it or your life will be forfeit." He went to Eventide next and threw the saddle on him as he spoke to Avril. "You will take my horse. He is much faster, but be careful with Chrisselle. She is too far along to be traveling."

"No, Ryce! I will not leave your side," Chrisselle cried, clutching his arm.

He growled, "You will not disobey me in this." When she would not let go, he stopped what he was doing and shook her roughly. "If ever there was a time to obey me this is it!"

Her eyes flashed with anger, but she answered softly. "Yes, Master."

Avril interrupted their exchange. "Ah wull leave ma horse, Bonnie, fur ye."

"Fine. I will join you only when I can assure you will not be harmed."

Chrisselle whimpered, "Don't leave me behind!"

"I *will* come back for you." He spoke to her motherly instincts, forcing her departure. "At this moment your duty is to protect our child."

She caressed her large stomach subconsciously. "I will, Ryce. I will protect our baby with my life."

He flinched. She could not know how her words cut him. "Leave now! Do not spare Eventide. Get to Avril's as fast as you can." He helped his extremely pregnant woman onto the horse with a feeling of foreboding.

Avril climbed up behind her. "Master Leon, Ah wull no fail ye or Mistress Leon."

He stroked her scarred cheek appreciatively. "I put my complete trust in you."

Chrisselle leaned over awkwardly to kiss him. "Come back to me, husband."

"Do not fret. I am capable of defending myself, pet." He backed away abruptly and shouted, "Now run!"

Eventide took off in a burst of speed. He watched them disappear into the trees and tried to calm his racing heart. It was happening all over again. Fate was cruel to replay his nightmare, but this time he refused to lose.

Ryce went back to the cottage and dressed for battle. Before he left the house, he picked up

Chrisselle's old leather collar and held it to his lips. *This will not be our end.*

He headed back to the barn and placed it in the chest along with his other mementoes. He slammed the lid down and locked it before carrying it into the woods. Ryce found a hiding place between two boulders and set it there for later retrieval.

Next, he brought Bonnie into the barn and secured her in Eventide's stall. Then he reentered the cottage and took down his claymore from the mantel. He made his stand in front of his home as the sun rays gently made their way over the landscape, warming the ground.

Ryce swung his sword in the air, readying his muscles for battle. He would put up a fight the likes of which they had never seen. He was a man of exceptional experience and skill. A man who was determined to defend what he had without the fear of death. Was there anything more dangerous in the world than he?

He heard the pounding of hooves as the horses crashed through the trees and he tensed, preparing himself for the hell about to ensue. *Death to all who would threaten me!* was his internal battle cry as the first of the rebels broke through the line of trees.

Soon fifty fully armed warriors surrounded him. This was not a simple uprising, this was a full-fledged rebellion. Ryce's stomach twisted. There would be no 'surviving' this.

"Sassenach filth!" a large burly Highlander spat. "Kiss the ground for it will be yur bed this night." Shouts and cheers echoed his statement.

"I come from England, but I have no quarrel with you," Ryce shouted above the din.

"All Sassenachs must die!" The leader looked to his comrades. "And all Sassenach sympathizers!"

Ryce tried to reason with the angry horde. "I detest the Baron as much as you. Hell, I will join you if it is your plan to overthrow the foul beast."

The Scotsman ignored him and roared, "First we kill his pet. Then we kill the master himself!"

For a moment Ryce believed they were talking about Chrisselle, until one of the men answered, "Tonight the Baron wull eat the same dirt as his Sassenach pet!"

Still determined to defuse the situation, Ryce encouraged them. "It is not necessary to shed blood today."

"Aye, but it is!" the leader shouted. "The de'il must be sent a bloody message."

The warriors descended on him as a unit. Ryce ducked and swerved, slicing at the horses' forelegs, causing several of them to stumble and fall, throwing the riders to the ground. He quickly disposed of two, but there were far too many men and they crushed around him, making his sword virtually useless. He felt the stab of metal into bone. Then his head exploded in pain as steel rebounded off his skull.

Ryce stumbled, but avoided another strike aimed at his head. He squeezed between the riders, trying to make room to make his stand. He looked up and found the broad-shouldered Scot leader before him. In a twisting motion, Ryce avoided the thrust of his attack and slashed open the man's thigh. The leader let out a cry of rage. One of his minions ran a sword through Ryce's stomach from behind.

Ryce fell to his knees, gasping for breath, the blood gushing from his head wound blinding him. The horses milled about as the warriors awaited their orders. The large Scot got off his horse and limped over to Ryce. "I shall gut the worthless pig."

Ryce's hands shook as he held his sword up in defense.

As two men advanced on him, Ryce growled in warning, ready to kill at least one before they disabled him. However, a handful of men came up from behind and easily wrestled the sword from his hands, forcing him to the ground. They each took an arm or leg and held him down.

Ryce took solace in the fact their leader was bleeding profusely and would soon be dead. The man knew it as well, and was determined to have his revenge before he drew his last breath. One of the men threw him a wicked knife made especially for butchering large animals. Ryce struggled out of instinct, but there was no escaping his fate.

He closed his eyes. This was how Jovita had met her end. It was grotesquely fitting.

"Sassenach swine. Feel my wrath!" The blade sank into his groin and a cold chill settled on him as the knife tugged and pulled its way through his stomach all the way to his sternum. His body shook uncontrollably and his breath came in violent gasps as the taste of blood filled his mouth.

Tears ran down his cheeks, not for his own pain but for the horror and pain he knew Jovita had suffered in her final moments. Blood gurgled from deep in his throat when he whispered, "I am sorry, love…"

"What was that, Sassenach filth?" the Scot shouted.

Ryce shook his head as the lights began to dim. He heard the agonized cries of Avril's horse as it was being slaughtered and then the smell of smoke filled the air. At least Chrisselle was safe. At least in that, he had not failed.

Ryce heard the voices of several men. He grasped for his sword, but his hand barely moved.

"He's still alive… somehow. I'll take him because you insist, but he will not live out the night."

Avril's sobs resonated in Ryce's head, but he could not open his eyes. "We wull no leave him!" she cried.

There was a horrifying jolt of pain when he was lifted and darkness took hold of him again. He woke next to the smell of fire. He struggled to move, afraid of the flames consuming him.

"Stay still," his pet's soothing voice purred. "You are hurt, but you are safe."

He relaxed and fell back into the darkness willingly, needing to escape from the searing pain.

When he regained consciousness again, he heard Avril and Chrisselle talking softly. "Master Leon telt ye to protect the bairn. Ye must rest."

"I cannot leave him, Avril. Master will awaken. I know he will."

Avril's voice became somber. "He cannae last the night."

"You don't know Master. He is stronger than you think. He will survive this!"

"Nae." Avril's tone was low and angry now. "Chrisselle, yer duty is tae care fur the babe. Ah wull wake ye if he stirs. Dinnae dishonor Master Leon's last wish by hurting the bairn. He needs tae die at peace. Tae ken ye and the babe ar healthy. Ye owe him that."

"Aye," Chrisselle said quietly. "But…"

"No!" Avril snapped. "If Master Leon wakes, tell him ye ar strong enough tae let him gae."

Ryce fell into fitful slumber, his body too damaged to remain aware. Later he woke to his own groaning. "I'm here, Ryce," Chrisselle whispered lovingly. "I will not leave you."

He forced his eyes open and croaked, "It is good to see you, pet."

She whimpered and tears formed in her eyes. Avril came into his line of vision. "Master Leon, Chrisselle is safe, the babe is well and the coins hidden. You hae nothin' tae worry about. Yer family wull live haur wi' me. We wull all be fine."

Ryce turned his head slowly to her and attempted a smile, but only half his face responded. "My Avril." He held up his hand and she grasped it. "I am well pleased."

Avril's lip trembled, but she swallowed hard and kissed his hand dutifully. "It is ma pleasure, Master Leon."

"Chrisselle," he rasped.

Avril moved away and Chrisselle rejoined him. "Avril will look out for you and the child. Share the coins with her. It will be enough…" He coughed up a large amount of blood and Chrisselle suddenly looked terrified. She needed his reassurance.

"Remember you are my wife, strong and beautiful. You will raise our child to be the same. Trust your instincts and do not let others sway you. *You* are her mother."

"Master…"

He suffered a terrible coughing fit that left him unable to speak and the darkness descended. Ryce fought against it, but did not awaken until later.

He saw Avril asleep in a chair by the fireplace. The instant he turned his head, he found Chrisselle looking down on him.

She took his hand and smiled. "You're back."

"Chrisselle, our babe needs you to rest."

"You need me."

He closed his eyes. If it had just been Avril and Chrisselle, he might have chanced remaining with them and recovering, trusting they would keep his secret. However, MacPherson had seen the extent of his injuries. The whole community must know of the attack by now. Anything less than his death would be met with fear and distrust. He had experienced it before, it would not happen again. There was only one option with Chrisselle unable to travel; he must die so that she and their baby could live.

He opened his eyes and sighed. "I don't want to leave you."

She fought back a sob and put his hand against her cheek. "I love you, Master."

"Ryce."

A single tear ran down her cheek. "I love you, Ryce."

"I love you, Chrisselle. I always will."

"No… please."

"Be brave, my pet."

More tears ran silently down her cheeks, but she nodded.

"You are a strong woman. Strong enough to survive alone and raise our daughter."

She shook her head. "It's a boy."

"Possibly," he conceded, "but promise me that *if* it is a girl you will name her Mae after my mother."

She gently lowered his hand and squeezed it lightly. "Yes, Ryce. I will name her Mae."

"You can depend on Avril but should you struggle, seek out Kegan. She is a good mother and I believe she will help you."

Chrisselle whispered with pain in her voice, "I will."

"My wife, I do not give my love lightly. Lean on it whenever you have need, it can never die."

"Aye, Ryce…" she choked.

"Hold strong to your hope. It will see you through the trying times ahead." He motioned her closer. "I am praying fate will see fit to bring a worthy mate into your life. I desire you to marry again."

"I'll have no other," she declared angrily.

"Pet," he corrected, "although you are capable of surviving on your own, life will be more agreeable if you are partnered. You may have to instruct him in your preferences, but it can be done humbly."

Her eyes betrayed her true response.

"Chrisselle, you were not meant to be alone. Do not pine for what was, you must live for the future… for you and our child." He gasped as a shooting pain coursed through his body. After a deep breath he added, "Let me go."

Her voice was filled with anguish. "Master, please don't leave me." Tears fell unhindered and she started sobbing quietly.

She had had a difficult pregnancy as it was and he feared for her health. "You must put our baby before your own needs. Rest now, Chrisselle. Do this for me."

"Please, Master."

He lifted his bloody hand slowly and caressed her cheek, leaving a red streak. "Do as I command."

She shook her head, but stood up and walked over to Avril's bed, curling up on it while staring at him sadly.

"My good wife. My loyal pet."

She gave him a gentle smile.

Ryce closed his eyes and waited. He waited until her soft rhythmic breath reached his ears. Even though the pain was excruciating, he slid off the table and made his way out with the two women sleeping deeply from exhaustion. He dragged himself to the barn.

Eventide nickered when he heard his master. "Yes, it is me, old friend." Ryce leaned against the gate and ignored the pain as he stroked the long neck of his steed. "You must stay." The horse stamped his hoof in protest.

"Stay, Eventide, because I cannot. Chrisselle will need you."

A racking cough threatened to give away his exodus. As much as he didn't want this, he patted his steed one last time. "You have been a good friend. I shall not forget your faithful service."

Ryce looked towards the cottage and sighed heavily before disappearing into the night. He headed straight for MacPherson's farm, picking the best horse for himself and releasing the others. By the time they rounded up the animals he would be far from the area.

He returned to his burned-out residence to retrieve the chest. It took time and concentration to overcome the agonizing pain as he lifted and strapped it to the saddle. He was overwhelmed by dizziness and almost blacked out.

Ryce was forced to lie on the ground to recover. Looking up at the stars, he coughed violently and wiped the blood from his lips. He stared at the red smear on his hand dazedly. *Jovita…*

He concentrated on the stars again, not allowing himself to go there. Jovita had loved the stars, believing they were the spirits of the past looking down on mankind with benevolence. *Are you up there, love?*

Ryce allowed himself to think back on those last days. Her swelling stomach, the radiance of her face as they both marveled at the miracle inside her. Her sweet, trilling laughter. He closed his eyes. Ryce felt the warmth of her hand as she placed his hand over her stomach and he felt the movement of it inside her.

Without warning, the streak of crimson flooded his brain again, her body opened from chest to groin, and *it* lying beside her. The tiny hands and feet perfect, eyes closed as if in sleep… their child, their baby boy.

Ryce held back the tears. Even after all that time the pain of her loss, of their hopes held in those tiny hands, cut like a fiery dagger in his heart.

Despite his condition, he forced himself back up and crawled onto the horse. That would not be Chrisselle's fate. She would live a full life, know the joy of birth and the satisfaction of raising her child. He would see to it.

Good Morrow

With the determination of the damned, Ryce turned away from the life he had built. He headed, instead, to the small cave where he had spent his first night with Chrisselle. As he lay on the cold ground in the gloomy hollow, he was accosted with memories of her. The girl had seemed so frail back then, too close to death to even survive a night. He chuckled softly, causing a spasm of hacking.

He shook his head when it passed. Chrisselle had proven him wrong. Her spirit was mightier than her body. He remembered threatening her when she wouldn't eat, and then having to feed her. It was the beginning of them. He'd fought hard to keep his distance, but Chrisselle's curiosity and vulnerability had eventually won him over.

Eventide had known it from the beginning. The horse was an old soul encased in an equine shell. It was regrettable that he had to leave his friend behind, but it gave Ryce solace to know Chrisselle would be looked after by the beast. He suspected she would find comfort in caring for the steed as well.

Ryce spent weeks healing from the massive wounds. After completing this final task, he would leave Scotland forever. He rode only at night to avoid others on the road. It made the trip longer, but he was in no hurry. The only thing that mattered was succeeding in his last endeavor.

The sweet, sickening stench of death surrounded the Baron's manor. The revolting aroma assaulted his nostrils before he came upon the bodies hanging from the trees lining the manor. The men were bloated, their faces frozen in various expressions of agony. A warning to others who would attempt to dethrone Sir Ryan of Rannoch. It was a grisly threat, but Ryce took consolation in the fact that the men who tried to end his own life were now swinging from trees. Noticeably missing was the burly Scot leader. It gratified Ryce to know the man had never made it to the Baron.

He dismounted and continued on foot. Where fifty men had failed, Ryce would succeed because he was not rash or emotional. He was a patient man.

The night Sir Ryan had taken Chrisselle, Ryce had promised himself the man would pay with his life for the deed. But it had been necessary to wait until there was no chance of harm coming to her.

There was nothing holding him back now. Ryce relished the thought that the Baron was feeling secure having just annihilated the rebellion. It was his overconfidence that made this easy. Ryce was able to enter the manor through the servants' entrance after skirting the guards. He stealthily navigated the dark manor up to the Baron's quarters.

To his disgust, when he opened the inner chamber door he saw the Baron humping a young maiden. He snuck behind the large bed and put his fingers to his lips when the girl glanced in his direction. Her eyes grew wide, but she said nothing.

Ryce pulled the rope from his pocket, then with swift grace he placed it over Sir Ryan's head and pulled it tight around his neck. The man fell backwards and off of the girl, who scrambled to the corner. She stifled her scream as she watched in rapt fascination.

Ryce kept it taut as he tied one end of the rope to the post of the bed and then did the same with the other. The rope was tight enough to constrict, but not enough to kill. He pulled out more rope and tied down the Baron's legs.

Then he stood above him and pulled out his claymore from the sheath. The Baron struggled underneath knowing there was no escape. Ryce understood his fear, having purposely orchestrated it to be reminiscent of his own attack. However, he would be swift.

"For my wife and all those you have harmed." Ryce thrust the sword into his heart. Sir Ryan shuddered once and then became still as the light slowly ebbed from his eyes.

Death never thrilled Ryce, but there were times when it was absolutely necessary. He nodded to the girl, who looked as if she was staring at the devil himself. Ryce appreciated that he must look like a ghoul with the gashes on his face and limbs.

At least she'd remained silent.

He exited the way he came and made it to his horse without any warnings being sounded. As he headed away from the manor, thoughts of Chrisselle assailed him. Her smile, her soft trilling laugh, the collar around her neck as she knelt before him.

He pushed the thoughts back and kicked the horse to move faster, but he could not run away from the visions invading his mind. Her soulful green eyes, those rose-colored lips, the feminine perfection of her mound. He closed his eyes and imagined himself deep inside her, with Chrisselle making those soft mewing sounds in the heat of passion…

I cannot lose her.

Ryce realized he loved her as deeply as his first love, Jovita. This was his chance to taste a normal life. He had been given an opportunity to witness his child being born, to be a part of raising a family.

Why am I running?

He would steal Chrisselle away and they would escape back to his motherland to build a new life. His heart pumped in his chest as Ryce slapped the reins of the horse and galloped at a breakneck speed back to her. A feeling of elation he had never known filled his being.

Chrisselle was the answer to his curse. He had simply been blind.

Ryce had an overabundance of funds back in England. He could make it work. They would have to wait a few months once the child was born before they could travel. His mind raced as he planned out every detail of the trip.

He made it to Avril's just before daybreak. Jumping off the winded beast, he headed straight for the cottage. Just before he made it to the door, Ryce heard a baby's cry. It stopped him in his tracks.

Chrisselle's sing-song voice soon followed. "There, there, Mae…" She began softly crooning a Scottish lullaby. "Baloo, baloo, my wee wee thing.

For thou art doubly dear to me. Thy daddie now is far awa'…"

Ryce took two steps back. Reality crashed over him like an icy wave. How could he condemn his family to his nomadic existence and rip them from the community that had embraced them?

Never safe, always moving. To doom Chrisselle and their tiny infant to that desperate lifestyle was selfish and cruel. If they survived the constant uprooting, he would still be forced to watch them grow old and die—tragic for him and horribly unfair to them.

This was his curse alone to suffer.

Ryce took two more steps back, fighting the overpowering urge to burst through the door and gather Chrisselle into his arms, to peek into the eyes of his newborn.

Do not condemn them to your fate.

With a will of iron, he turned around and returned to the horse. He took the reins, unbuckled the bridle and let it slip to the ground. Ryce unloaded the chest and then slapped the animal on the haunches. "Go home," he commanded. The beast snorted once before heading in the direction of MacPherson's farm.

He heard Eventide nicker for him from the barn at the sound of his voice, but Ryce ignored the steed's call. His duty was to remain dead and allow his family to live on in peace. He had been wrong to come back.

Ryce picked a dew-covered sprig of heather just opening to the rays of the brilliant sunrise bursting forth in the east. He laid it down at the threshold and touched the wooden door that separated him from his family. He could hear the soft cooing sounds of his daughter on the other side. He whispered, "Good morrow, Chrisselle and my wee Mae."

He lifted the chest up off the ground and hoisted it onto his back.

A good time to die.

Ryce could not return to England—not after this. He needed to travel far from this continent. Someplace foreign and untried would help ease the loss. This time, unlike the past, he had the peace of knowing Chrisselle and their tiny daughter were alive and well.

It was… enough.

Coming in 2014

Dom of the Ages is the continuing series following the many lives and loves of Ryce Leon – a man of all ages.

You can find Red on:

Twitter: @redphoenix69
Website: RedPhoenix69.com
Facebook: Red Phoenix

Red Phoenix is the author of:

Brie Learns the Art of Submission
* Available in eBook and paperback

(Submissive Exploration—A young woman enters a world of new experiences when she enrolls in the Submissive Training Center)

———————————

Brie Embraces the Heart of Submission
* Available in eBook and Paperback

(Submission of the Heart—After being collared, Brie learns that submission is sexier and more challenging than she'd ever imagined)

———————————

Blissfully Undone

* Available in eBook and paperback

(Snowy Fun—Two people find themselves snowbound in a cabin where hidden love can flourish, taking one couple on a sensual journey into ménage à trois)

Sensual Erotica: The Erotic Love Story of Amy and Troy

* Available in eBook and paperback

(Sexual Adventures—True love reigns, but fate continually throws Troy and Amy into the arms of others)

(Novellas and Novelettes available as eBooks)

Novellas

His Scottish Pet: Dom of the Ages

(Scottish Dom—A sexy Dom escapes to Scotland in the late 1400s. He encounters a waif who has the potential to free him from his tragic curse)

Varick: The Reckoning

(Savory Vampire—A dark, sexy vampire story. The hero navigates the dangerous world he has been thrust into with lusty passion and a pure heart)

Novelettes

Keeper of the Wolf Clan
(Sexual Secrets—A virginal werewolf must act as the
clan's mysterious Keeper)

In 9 Days
(Sweet Romance—A young girl falls in love with the
new student, nicknamed 'the Freak')

---

9 Days and Counting
(Sacrificial Love—The sequel to In 9 Days delves
into the emotional reunion of two longtime lovers)

And Then He Saved Me
(Saving Tenderness—When a young girl tries to kill
herself, a man of great character intervenes with a
love that heals)

Play With Me at Noon
(Seeking Fulfillment—A desperate wife lives out her
fantasies by taking five different men in five days)

Connect with Red on Substance B

Substance B is a new platform for independent authors to directly connect with their readers. Please visit Red's Substance B page (substance-b.com/RedPhoenix.html) where you can:

- Sign up for Red's newsletter
- Send a message to Red
- See all platforms where Red's books are sold

Visit Substance B today to learn more about your favorite independent authors.

Made in the USA
Columbia, SC
19 July 2020

14163852R00105